BERNARD LAZARE

THE TORCH-BEARERS

TRANSLATED AND WITH AN INTRODUCTION BY
BRIAN STABLEFORD

Contents

Introduction

LES PORTEURS DE TORCHES by Bernard Lazare, here translated as *The Torch-Bearers*, was published by Armand Colin et Cie in 1897. That was five years after his first collection of short stories, *Le Miroir des légendes* (1892; tr. as *The Mirror of Legends* in a Snuggly Books edition of 2017), but only a matter of months before his third and last, *La Porte d'ivoire* (dated 1897 but actually 1898; tr. as *The Gate of Ivory*) which was advertised in the preliminary pages of *Les Porteurs de torches* as "*sous presse*" [in press]. It is probable that the two Armand Colin volumes were prepared and submitted simultaneously, and that their order of publication was a matter of marketing strategy rather than a reflection of the order of composition.

Ordinarily, the exact order of the composition of the elements of two short story collections, whose contents were probably composed over a period of years, would be a trivial issue, but in this particular instance it has a considerable bearing on the interpretation of the two Colin volumes, neither of which is a simple miscellany of previously-published materials, and each of which seems to mark a distinct stage in the author's philosophical development. Although it does contain a sequence of short stories, *Les Porteurs de torches* is certainly not a simple assemblage;

the stories are contained within an elaborate frame-narrative, in which context they are represented as serving a definite and highly idiosyncratic illustrative purpose.

The stories in the companion volume, *La Porte d'ivoire*, are also unified by a narrative frame of sorts, and even more so by a common method of construction similar to that employed in *Les Porteurs de torches*—which is to say that they are almost all presented as stories within stories, told by a narrator with the ostensible purpose of illustrating a philosophical argument. The link between the two collections is further emphasized by the fact that the narrator of most of the stories in *La Porte d'ivoire*—or all of them, at least tacitly—has the same name as one of the leading characters in the frame-narrative of *Les Porteurs des torches*, although he is not the same person.

The reason why the relationship of *Les Porteurs de torches* to its companion volume—and, for that matter, to its predecessor—is important is that the frame-narrative of the portmanteau is a story about story-telling, which embodies an analysis and a critique of the manner in which stories are composed, and their innate purpose. That critique is, at least in part, scathing, and could be read as a harsh judgment on the manner and purpose of the stories contained in the other two collections. Indeed, that judgment seems so harsh, in sum, that it might easily give the impression that it could only lead to a capital sentence: a renunciation by the author of writing stories of that type, and perhaps any stories at all. If it were to be assumed that the whole of *La Porte d'ivoire* was composed before the text of *Les Porteus de torches* was completed—as might, in fact, be the case—then *Les Porteurs de torches* could appear to constitute an effective resignation letter on the part of the author, at least from the Symbolist Movement, at whose core he had been when he wrote *Le Miroir de légendes*, one of the most archetypal prose products of that Movement, and perhaps from writing any fiction at all.

That was clearly not the author's intention, however. As well as advertising the impending publication of *La Porte d'ivoire*, the preliminary material of *Les Porteurs de torches* also advertised a novel, *Les Ames obscures* [Obscure Souls], as "en preparation," so Lazare certainly intended, at that point in time, to continue writing fiction, and had work of that kind in progress. In fact, that novel never appeared. Perhaps it was finished, but was not published because the author's first three works of fiction had sold too poorly; perhaps, on the other hand, the author never managed to finish it, his impetus somewhat undermined by the apparent self-criticism contained in *Les Porteurs des torches*. No one knows now, and perhaps no one ever did, including Bernard Lazare—but that very uncertainty helps to make *Les Porteurs des torches* a highly unusual and extraordinarily intriguing text.

The Snuggly Books edition of *The Mirror of Legends* contains an overall account of Bernard Lazare's life and career, of which it is only necessary here to offer a brief synopsis. He was born Lazare Bernard on 14 June 1865 in Nîmes in the south of France, and went to Paris in October 1886 at the behest of his friend Georges Michel, who had preceded him there in 1883. Michel was part of Stéphane Mallarmé's circle of acolytes, who formed the core of the burgeoning Symbolist Movement, and he published poetry and prose as Ephraïm Mikhail; he and Lazare became the central figures in their own subsidiary clique, the "Moineaux francs" [house sparrows]. Lazare also became a regular at one of the Movement's other major cénacles, the salon hosted by José-Maria de Heredia, and he befriended the aged Comte de Villiers de l'Isle Adam, now fallen on exceedingly hard times but still a legendary hero to all young writers of "Decadent literature"—a description initially coined by Désire Nisard in the 1830s as an insult aimed at Romantic writers, but adopted with pride by the more radical practitioners of literary *romanticisme*, assertively retained by several of the promoters of post-Romantic *avant gardes*, and worn with particular pride by many of the Symbolists.

Lazare's position at the heart of the Symbolist Movement retained his wholehearted commitment for a number of years; he published prolifically in Symbolist periodicals between 1887 and 1893, when all of the material in *Le Miroir des légendes* was written. Lazare's literary activity was already broadening out, however, by virtue of political and philosophical interests that he only shared with a minority of his fellow Symbolists—a tiny minority in respect of his strong interest in the history and cultural situation of Judaism, which became even tinier when Georges Michel died of tuberculosis in 1890. Superficially, at least, the interest taken by one sector of the Movement in Anarchism seemed a much larger minority—it would have been difficult in the early 1890s to throw a stone into any Parisian literary salon without hitting a self-declared Anarchist—but in fact, the appellation was often an affectation. In Lazare's case, it was not, and his numerous journalistic contributions to Anarchist periodicals showed a rare intellectual commitment and analytical fervor, of which *Les Porteurs de torches* was the most elaborate fruit.

Although it would be an exaggeration to say the *Les Porters des torches* is the only work by a member of the Symbolist Movement to exhibit Anarchist convictions elaborately and insistently, it is by far and away the most remarkable. Its primary purpose is to examine the question of what Anarchist fiction might actually be like, in terms of the narrative devices that it ought to use, and it is, in essence, a striking literary experiment, testing the hypothesis that the raw materials of myth, legend and folklore, which had been redeployed and pastiched so successfully by the Symbolists, could be adapted to Anarchist purposes. It is written in the awareness that the reflexive assumption made by many writers and critics might be negative, but with a certain natural inclination to resist that conclusion.

The first major product of Lazare's interest in Judaism was his analytical history of *L'Antisémitisme, son histoire et ses causes* (1894; tr. as. *Anti-Semitism, its History and its Causes*), which has not the slightest sympathy with anti-semitism, but whose attempts to explain the phenomenon seemed to some readers be lending fuel to it, and led to continual repetition of the absurd charge that Lazare was himself anti-semitic—an accusation that continued to haunt his reputation for the rest of his life and long after his death. That interest played a key part in what was to become Lazare's major political involvement, which began when he wrote an article in 1896 about the awful treatment meted out by the French army and the French political establishment to Captain Alfred Dreyfus, the victim of a trumped-up charge of treason that various tribunals insisted in upholding long after his innocence became abundantly clear. Lazare's article ended with the ringing phrase "J'accuse," which was subsequently employed as a headline by Émile Zola, and effectively launched the so-called "Dreyfus Affair," which raged in Paris for the next decade.

The fact that Lazare published no more fiction after 1898 probably has at least as much do with his intense involvement in campaigning on behalf of Dreyfus than any after-effect of the apparent disillusionment measured and specified in *Les Porteurs de torches*. He died before the Affair was concluded, on 1 September 1903, following surgery that attempted to remove a malignant tumor from his bowel. There were, however, other complicating factors in his life that limited his literary production after 1892. In that year he finally married Isabelle Grumbach, with whom he had been romantically linked since they had met in Nîmes as teenagers, and who had followed him to Paris, supporting herself there by working in Nadar's photographic studio. His family had always opposed the relationship, refused to attend the wedding and effectively cut him off thereafter, surrounding the couple with a hostility to which Lazare always reacted defiantly; *Les Porteurs des torches*, in bearing the dedication: "To my wife," is not making a banal sentimental reference, and one of the things that its frame narrative and contained narratives have in common with all of Lazare's fiction is the equivocally defensive tension of their attitude to amour.

Amour is not by any means the only subject viewed through the literary lens of *Les Porteurs des torches* in an equivocal manner, and its ambiguities extend in several respects to a deliberate mystification that was a significant clause in several of the Symbolist manifestoes issued by the members of the Movement. Superficially, its "plot" is quite simple: An itinerant Anarchist preacher comes to the corrupt city of Geronta in the company of a fellow vagabond, where he begins preaching in parables, that being his preferred method of enlightenment. He hears a number of other story-tellers narrating their own parables, to which he opposes his own in order to expose their ideological flaws. He attracts a small number of followers won over to his way of thinking, but his career is eventually brought to its logical and inevitable conclusion. That superficial simplicity, however, overlays several puzzling complications.

The first of those puzzles is the preacher himself, whose identity seems to change somewhat in the course of the story. In the first chapter he seems to have come from another world, entirely foreign to some of the concepts that his fellow vagabond employs, including the concept of property, but he subsequently implies that his adventure in Geronta is merely a repetition of a pattern of events that has happened to him many times before. At times he seems to be recapitulating the career of Jesus, but at others he assimilates "the vagabond of Galilee" to the evil that he is trying to oppose, accusing him forthrightly of being part of the problem rather than a solution. His name is Marcus, but that name was certainly not chosen as an echo of Marx—Karl Marx was not an Anarchist—and there are several hints dropped in the story that it actually echoes the name of the Evangelist Mark.

It cannot be emphasized too heavily that the frame narrative of the portmanteau, like the stories it contains, is a parable and an exercise in symbolism; Geronta is certainly an analogue of Paris, but it is not Paris; it is a symbol of Paris. The Symbolist writer Anselme is an analogue of the Anselme who serves as a narrator of the stories in *La Porte d'ivoire*, who is in turn an analogue of Lazare himself, but he is not the same person. Perhaps the most significant implication of that kind of symbolic regress is not the veiled suggestion that Marcus is in some sense a version of the Evangelist Mark, but rather that the Evangelist Mark is a version of Marcus: not a reporter but a fabulist, and that the story of Jesus the maker of parables its itself a parable. It is undoubtedly significant that the references to Mark within *Les Porteurs de Torches* connect him to the Gnostic tradition of early Christian belief—a tradition featured in more than one of the tales told within the story by tellers to whom Marcus is opposed.

The comparison of *Les Porteurs de torches* with *La Porte d'ivoire* is illuminating in several ways, but most obviously in the fact that the tale told therein by Anselme prior to his enlightenment by Marcus is strongly reminiscent of several of the tales in the companion collection, both in its story-arc and its specific symbolism. It is a kind of story that is very abundantly represented in the core canon of Symbolist prose, reproducing a pattern frequently seen in the more conspicuously Decadent fabulations of such writers as Catulle Mendès, Jean Lorrain and the early work of Lazare's friend Henri de Régnier. It would, however, be a mistake to construe Anselme's subsequent change of heart in *Les Porteurs de torches* as a rejection of Symbolism. It is certainly not a rejection of Symbolist narrative strategy, which Marcus employs himself and considers crucial to his endeavor, and nor, for the same reason, can it be considered a rejection of Symbolist ambiguity, or of the typically melancholy aspect of Decadent consciousness that Baudelaire had called *spleen* and Maurice Magre was later to call, more forthrightly, *désespoir* [despair]. If Marcus insists on conserving hope for the Anarchist Millennium, and wants to insist that Anselme—and, tacitly, the readers that the story is attempting to propagandize—should conserve it too, he does so with tears in his eyes that will never dry up; he is, quintessentially, a martyr to his cause.

It is worth observing that Lazare was not the only Anarchist who attempted to adapt fabular parables to the evangelizing of his political faith, and that a particularly interesting comparison can be made between his work in that vein and the work of Henri Ner (1861-1938), who changed the orthography of his name in 1898 to Han Ryner, when he decided that all his future writing would be committed to the Anarchist cause. Ryner produced two volumes of fabular parables, *Las Voyages de Psychodore, philosophe cynique* (1903; tr. as "The Travels of Psychodore, Cynic Philosopher") and *Les Paraboles cyniques* (1913; tr. as "Cynic Parables"), specifically arguing in the introduction to the latter that the use of parables as a teaching method had been pioneered by the cynic philosophers, and that the complete loss of their writings as partly due to deliberate neglect by Christian copyists intent on maintaining an unjustified monopoly. Although Ryner made no reference to Lazare in that essay, it would be surprising if he had not read *Les Porteurs de torches* and had not thought long and hard about the implications of its argument, even though he, unlike Marcus, was not at all unwilling to indulge in futuristic speculation and utopian design.

Les Porteurs de torches was not, therefore, a work without influence, and its argument ought not seen as a kind of terminus, attempting to bring down the curtain of the kind of literary endeavor to which its author had previously dedicated his life. It is at least possible, and perhaps probable, that some of the stories in *La Porte d'ivoire* were written alongside or after the elements of its companion portmanteau, and there is no reason to think that if Lazare had been able to continue writing for as long as Ryner that he would not have produced a good deal more fiction, continuing the evolution from the "pure" symbolism of *Le Miroir des légendes* in the direction of greater philosophical and narrative complexity, and more determined political commitment.

It would have been difficult to produce and publish such works, surrounded by multiple hostilities as Lazare was, but he would have done it, even with tears in his eyes. The fact that he could not is cause for regret, because the arguments raised in *Les Porteurs de torches* regarding the esthetic and intellectual utility of fabular parables really are important questions. There is certainly one sense in which the literary experiment might seem to the reader to have failed, in that Marcus' parables, precisely because they deliberately discard many of the rhetorical tricks of conventional fiction, seem so alien as hardly to qualify as "stories" at all, but the whole point of them is to make the reader think about aspects of reading that might have been too readily taken or granted before, and an invitation at least to take an interest, if not to rejoice, in seeing that mold broken.

The following translation was made from the copy of the 1897 Armand Colin edition reproduced on the Bibliothèque Nationale's *gallica* website.

—Brian Stableford

THE TORCH-BEARERS

I

The Encounter

THE MAN had probably been walking for a long time. His shoes, once sturdy, were split, and the sharp pebbles of the roads had made large wounds in them. His clothes were wretched; the inhumane brambles of the pathways, the teeth of dogs, and also those of pitchforks, had ripped his trousers and lacerated the shabby frock-coat that covered his meager shoulder-blades.

As he was on the edge of a wood he sat down on the moss at the foot of a tree and decided to await hazard there. It was spring; the sky was limpid and calm, the sun was only smiling as yet, and the cool air was rendering the poor fellow's limbs listless. The moment being propitious, he began to dream.

Perhaps he dreamed about feasting, for the famished are often imaginative and take pleasure in substituting visions for reality; but while awaiting the meat that his fantasy promised, the wanderer chewed some deceptive bark mechanically, perhaps trying, by means of that futile mastication, to calm the aching of his stomach.

Around him, the silence was immense, the plain quiet and the forest mute, and the vagabond, understanding the lessons of the great mother, fell asleep. He slept for a long time, and would doubtless have slept even longer if he had not been prevented from doing so by the touch of a hand tapping his shoulder.

He sat up, rubbed his swollen eyes, and said, simply: "I believe you were wrong to wake me up."

"I'm sure of it," replied the untimely individual who was confronting the sleeper, "for sleep is a good thing, which brings forgetfulness."

"Very true," retorted the vagabond, and he examined the intruder curiously.

He was a man of fairly tall stature, thin, with drooping shoulders. He wore a long beard, almost unkempt, which hid the form of his face completely, in which one could only see a slightly curved nose and two bright and luminous eyes. He was shod in solid boots, beaten by the flaps of a vast overcoat with Brandenburg buttons, which enveloped him entirely. A bulging sack was slung over his shoulder, and his hands were resting on a cane with a curved handle as he gazed at his interlocutor.

"Would you care to sit down, then?" said the latter,

"With pleasure," he said, "and if you like, we can chat; but before then, permit me to share some victuals with you."

So saying, he took out of his sack bread, cheese, fruits and a few accessories, which the vagabond devoured gluttonously.

"Are you bulimic?" asked the host, surprised.

"No," replied the wretch, "just hungry." And he resumed eating.

"You astonish me," the other went on. "I met a serious man on the road yesterday who demonstrated to me that one cannot suffer from hunger in your country."

"He must have been an economist," opined the starveling.

"What do you call an economist?"

"A licensed citizen who has the difficult but rewarding responsibility of proving to the poor the legitimacy and mildness of their estate."

"Are there many of those men among you?"

"Too many, Monsieur, for, as soon as a merchant, an industrialist or a financier has acquired a fortune he only has one objective: to justify it; and he becomes an economist, unless he prefers to devote himself to philanthropy, a delightful profession that permits him to bandage for the second half of his life the wounds he inflicted in the first."

"And what are you, then?"

"I'm an educated man, Monsieur, begging your pardon."

"I'm delighted to hear it, Monsieur; but what is your condition,"

"Poor."

"Why poor?"

"Because I have nothing."

The man with the long beard seemed perplexed. One might have thought that it was the first time he had heard anything similar said, and that the words that had just been pronounced had no meaning for him.

"Excuse me if I'm importuning you," he said, "but what do you mean by the expression: *have nothing?*"

"It means, benevolent foreigner, that I don't possess anything, that I'm not an owner."

"A curious country."

"Do you know one that is different?"

"I can imagine one where everything belongs to every-one."

"A utopian conception, Monsieur. But forgive me, while still entirely stuffed with your benefits, for daring to contradict you. In order to comprehend our customs, then, suppose that everything belongs to a few."

"Strange," said the man.

"That surprises you?"

"What surprises me is your admirable resignation. Why don't you reclaim a part of what is detained by that minority?"

"Because we respect property," replied the vagabond, proudly.

"Prodigious!" exclaimed the stranger. "So you can't take possession of another's property?"

"Certainly not."

"And if you're dying of hunger?"

"Honor commands us to perish rather than steal."

"Honor . . . steal . . . what does that mean?"

"Monsieur, you're nothing but a barbarian. Honor consists of observing a series of conventions that we haven't made, and from which we generally suffer, but which it's important, so it's said, to maintain for the common good. As for stealing, it's the action by which one takes possession of one's neighbor's property. It's recommended not to infringe honor and not to practice stealing."

"Stealing is punished, then?"

"Yes, when the thief doesn't posses anything."

"When does one possess something?"

"When one has stolen a great deal."

"I don't understand."

"It's quite simple, though. Would you like me to tell you my story?"

"Please do."

"Here it is. It's short, vulgar, and will also illustrate admirably what I say. I was orphaned very young, at the age of five, and my father, who only survived my mother by two years, confided me to one of his oldest friends, a venerable, austere and esteemed man who lived in a rather remote provincial town. My guardian brought me up in the best principles, inculcated me with the soundest laws of morality, and did not leave me ignorant of any of my duties. He taught me that wealth is pernicious and honorable poverty looked upon kindly by Heaven.

"In order to help me understand the excellence of those aphorisms practically, until the age of fifteen he gave me five sous every fortnight, in order to devote myself to the pleasures of my age. I always thought that he attributed a cabalistic influence to the number five and its multiples.[1] At any rate, he had me given a good education in the schools of the capital. When I was twenty-one years old I returned to my birthplace.

"There my guardian deigned to inform me that the paternal patrimony had been barely sufficient to pay for my education, and that he had been obliged to provide, personally, the fortnightly subsidies that his generosity had attributed to me. He concluded his little speech by engaging me urgently to understand the gravity of my situation, and told me no longer to count on him.

"I was surprised, for I was not unaware that my father had left a rather considerable fortune. I sought information from the family notary; that upright lawyer declared that I had been told the sad truth, but he gave me evidence in

---

1 The French term equivalent to the English "fortnight" is *quinzaine*, literally "fifteen days," hence the remark about multiples of five.

which the deceit of which I had been the victim appeared to me clearly."

"Your story isn't dramatic, my friend," the stranger interjected, "but it's instructive. Tell me, then, did your guardian not have any respect for property?"

"Him! Let me continue. Ruined, devoid of all resources and deprived of assistance, I resolved to quit that excessively remote region and, strong in my right and convinced of the legitimacy of my endeavor, on the night after our explanation, I made a small package of a few objects that were dear to me, broke into my guardian's strong-box, took a thousand-franc banknote that was to serve as traveling expenses, and fled at daybreak."

"You were not wrong."

"That was not the opinion of the man I left behind. He had no hesitation in setting the police on my heels. I was arrested, imprisoned, tried and sentenced, in spite of my efforts to make my case understood to the magistrates, who reproached me for having stolen the property of another. I spent two years in jail, and when the doors of the prison were opened to me, I saw all others closed. I was not unduly upset; I was already disgusted with the company of men, and I preferred begging for my bread to seeking in society for some ward to bring up."

"Your story has interested me, Monsieur, but it is filled with the most absurd contradictions, and, unless one supposes that you live in a land of good-for-nothings, I cannot believe what you tell me, nor that what is honored in your guardian has been so rudely punished in you."

"I could reply to you that my guardian was rich with my wealth and that I no longer had a fortune, which would be sufficient to explain many things, but . . . are you going to Geronta?" he interrogated, abruptly.

"Isn't that the capital of this country?"

"Yes."

"Then I'll certainly go."

"Well," said the poor wretch, "Go find someone that I knew there when I came out of prison. He's a young man well versed in sociology; he's a student or a professor at the Political School. I'll give you his name and address. See him; you'll obtain a profit from his conversation. He'll enlighten you regarding all the contradictions in my story. He'll explain to you the mechanism of property and clarify the differences that separate proprietors, and you'll doubtless return to your fatherland satisfied."

"I have no fatherland, Monsieur."

"Allow me to admire you, but permit me to ask you who you are. We have habits of classification here that prevent us from leaving anyone outside fixed categories. Although, in the course of our numerous revolutions, castes have been abolished, it gives us satisfaction to put everyone in a determined pigeon-hole. We have an instinct and love of order."

"Before replying to you, I would like to ask you a question. Are people of your class numerous?"

"Wandering or sedentary, we are the majority," the vagabond declared, not without pride.

"You have a singular notion of order, then!"

"On the contrary, we have a very precise notion of it. Order consists of preventing my peers from attacking privileges and disrupting the established divisions; it also consists of persuading ourselves, if not of the excellence of our fate, at least the necessity of submission to it."

"Those are means of establishing a material order. You have a very precise sense of methods of political equilibrium, but, I repeat, you are ignorant of order and harmony. Let us leave it there, however. I make it a principle to conform everywhere to exterior customs, so classify me as you wish, if that makes things easier for you. Would you like to know my name?"

"Speak."

"My name is Marcus. Is your curiosity satisfied?"

"It will be if you so wish, but it would please me to know your homeland and your estate."

"Have I not told you that I am a citizen of the world? As for my estate, say, if you like, that I am an apostle of the human species, a procurer of the truth and an orator of justice."

"I see: you're a philosopher and a revolutionary, and by your questions you have doubtless abused my candor or simply wished to enlighten me. I don't hold that against you, and now that I know you, we can chat more advantageously. As for me, I've told you my story, and it only remains for me to tell you that my name is Juste."

"Have you a goal, Juste?"

"I have none except for the one natural to all existence."

"If you mean death, that isn't a goal but an end."

"Oh, you're pedantic, and it isn't appropriate to talk to you hyperbolically. In that case, I have no goal. I go straight ahead, southwards when winter is imminent, northwards when summer returns; that is the custom of the rich, so I have nothing to envy them."

"Would you like to be my guide?"

"Why not? Your sack appears to me to be full, and the experience I had just now proves to me that your provisions are acceptable. Now, I tell you cynically that, although accustomed often to live on pure air and fresh water, I'm always sensible to the allure of less hollow nourishment. You're offering me that, aren't you? Doubtless you wouldn't want your guide to be responsible for providing for his own needs."

"Certainly not. You accept, then?"

"That depends. Where are you going?"

"Haven't you engaged me to see Geronta? I'm curious to know that city."

"It's an interesting city, and after a few years of vagabondage, I'll return there with pleasure. So, Old Master—forgive my youth for addressing you thus—the journey pleases me, and I'm your man."

"Let's go," said Marcus.

He put the remains of the meal into his sack. Juste picked up the knotty stick that he never abandoned, and, as the sun was setting, they quit the woods in order to find lodgings before night fell; for the distance was still great between that peaceful forest and tumultuous Geronta.

"Are you a good walker?" Juste asked his companion at the moment of the departure.

"Yes," the philosopher replied.

"We'll be in Geronta in two days, then, at midday, and we can rest at the Inn of the Dove."

II

The Inn of the Dove

"WHY are people looking at us in that fashion?" Marcus asked Juste when they had passed through the gates of Geronta.

"Don't be wounded by the reply I'm going to make, Old Master: they're admiring your overcoat. An unfortunate overcoat, in that regard, and it will be necessary for you to quit the city quickly if you don't want to attract curiosity, but fortunate, on the other hand, if you intend to be known and to spread your doctrines, for here, in order for people to listen to you, it's first necessary to have an overcoat."

"It's the same everywhere, my friend, and Alicibiades once cut off his dog's tail in order to solicit the attention of the Athenians. As for me, it doesn't matter, and if I retain my overcoat, it's because it keeps me warm."

"I don't see any inconvenience in that," replied Juste. "I feared, I confess, that you might add a new chapter to *Sartor Resartus*[1]—not that it would have displeased me

---

1 Thomas Carlyle's eccentric work of fiction *Sartor Resartus* (serialized 1833-34) is a pretended commentary by an English "reviewer" on the life and thought of an imaginary German philosopher

12

to hear you, and I'm still ready to do so, but when we've entered the hospitable house you can see over there."

The house that Juste designated was of modest appearance; it was isolated in a little square and formed the spur of an island framed by two broad roads. Its surroundings were very busy and peasant carts could be seen entering and emerging from its large vault. Above the door was a sign in the middle of which a dove perched on a gilded sphere was painted.

"That's the Inn of the Dove," said Juste. "Excuse me for showing pleasure at the sight of it, but remember that I'm finally going to sit down at a table and eat hot food with a precise odor, served in large dishes whose sight alone satisfies the senses of those who, like me, are abstinent by necessity."

"I understand your pleasure, Juste; in similar circumstances I would once have shared it, and I have not reached an age that renders me indifferent to those satisfactions. I would not want to delay your pleasure, then. However, can you, who seem to be familiar with these places, explain the allegorical image displayed at the entrance to the inn?"

Juste was about to reply, but did not have the time; someone approached the philosopher, greeted him in an urbane manner and said: "Forgive me, Monsieur, for accosting you in a manner that might appear uncivil to you, but no one can reveal the meaning of that crude painting to you better than me. I penetrated the arcanum of it a few months ago, and since then, I have taken pleasure in roam-

---

supposedly renowned for having written a book on *Clothes: Their Origin and Influence*. While gently mocking German idealism and the Romanticism of Goethe, Carlyle employs the imaginary philosopher as a mouthpiece for uncomfortable truths. The analogy between that work and the present one is a trifle distant, but significant.

ing this square and playing, with regard to strangers—for my fellow citizens, alas, are unable to have concerns of that order—the role of initiator.

"Do you not see, Monsieur, that the dove in question is the spirit that, in spite of everything, dominates, governs and guides the world? What an admirable genius the naïve and unskillful artist who painted that panel possessed! He was undoubtedly ignorant even of the anatomy of the dove, but he wanted to give a lesson to some, and, at the very gates of this city devoted to matter, he has raised the protest of the spirit."

Marcus listened to the speaker and contemplated him. He was a beardless and thin adolescent with a pale face, sunken eyes, and long and slightly greasy hair. He was clad in a frock-coat almost as long as the overcoat admired by the passers-by, and he was leaning in an idle fashion on a cane whose pommel was an amethyst.

Juste looked at him ironically; when the speech ended, he struck his thigh forcefully while lifting his leg—which was a fashion of manifesting his satisfaction—and he started laughing.

"Why are you laughing?" asked Marcus.

"I'm laughing at the ingenuity of this young man and the adroit fashion in which he interprets images. He's certainly a clever symbolist! Would you like me to explain now the reasons that led the worthy founder of this house to adopt that sign?"

"Speak," replied Marcus.

"Once, on the very spot where this inn stands, stood the stall of the most famous conjurer in Geronta. He knew all the tricks with goblets, the finest and the most complicated in the world. He was also a subtle animal-handler;

he knew how to train dogs and monkeys, but the inmate of his establishment that charmed the idlers most was an educated pigeon. Nothing similar had ever been seen. That bird could carry burdens, and it was also able to light the fuses of little metal cannons, but the most brilliant of its exercises consisted of moving over an inclined plane a ball of gilded cardboard, which it rolled with its feet. It's the memory of that pigeon to which this naïve painting is consecrated."

"What do you say to that, Monsieur?" Marcus asked the mystagogue.

The mystagogue smiled scornfully, and, doubtless not caring to remain any longer in such stupid company, he drew away without deigning to respond.

"You see, Juste," the philosopher remarked, "how difficult it is to make people listen to the voice of reason. That encounter on the threshold of the city is significant; I'll willingly take it as a presage of what awaits me here, and the welcome that my neo-peripateticism will receive."

"I'll help you to support that, Old Master, but believe me, let's not remain motionless any longer before this door, cackling like crows. It seems to me that I chat better when I've had a drink."

Marcus consented with a gesture and followed his companion, who led him into the already bustling hall of the inn. There, an aged waitress made a sign of amity to Juste, who seemed pleased to be recognized after long years of absence; she had the two travelers sit down, and then hastened to serve them. Pleasure caused Juste's eyes to sparkle, for no one was more attached to the pleasures of the stomach than he was.

As for his friend, if he did not abstain from beans, he followed nevertheless the precepts of the Pythagoreans. He nourished himself on vegetables and milk and drank water, and if his knapsack contained any alcoholic liquor, it was only a cordial destined for any ailing individuals he might encounter on his road. Thus, he was insensible to the seductions of the Inn of the Dove. The odor of sauces and roast meat did not even make his nostrils twitch, whereas Juste's opened wide, as if they desired to absorb what his mouth could not savor. When he judged that the latter's satisfied appetite left his spirit liberated, he resumed the conversation.

"Does it not seem to you, Juste, that we treated that young stranger severely?"

"Did we address any disobliging words to him?"

"No, but you did worse, you mocked his philosophy."

"You call that a philosophy?"

"Certainly; isn't it an interpretation of things? That youth commented on images for us; be certain that he could just as easily have given us an interpretation of the world, departing from the same point. His method is also excellent, beyond all criticism because it only rests on his fantasy; it would be deplorable, I grant you, to guide us in the coordination of physical laws, but its principle might serve as the basis for a poetics."

"The poetics of symbolism."

"Exactly. I once knew a poet, completely forgotten since, but who had a sagacious and profound intelligence. He claimed that legend had been the frame into which humanity had put its hopes, its desires, its dreams, its dolors and its disappointments. According to him, in the course of the ages, under the influence of a few privileged castes that had an interest in adulterating significance, those myths had become insignificant amusements, old wives' tales and nursery narratives to which serious people no longer paid any attention, and we were no longer capable of rediscovering, beneath the veils that covered them, the verities contained in our ancestors' symbols."

"Doubtless your poet also claimed to be the veridical interpreter of those fables?"

"Naturally; he even had the custom of saying, like Athenaeus of Aeschylus: 'I alone have the keys to the divine chambers.'"

"Don't you think that was a singular folly on his part?"

"An error, at the most, even a double error, both historical and metaphysical. He was wrong to accord an absolute value to his exegesis and the extract dogmas from his interpretations. He was also mistaken in attributing such profound conceptions to our ancestors; in endowing them with his own intellectuality, he was acting like our young man, who sees the poor sign-painter as some elevated initiate.

"Our forefathers, like our savages, created deformed myths to explain phenomena, for they had the divine virtue without which humankind would still be crawling in darkness and fetid mud: curiosity. Their myths can only bring us one testimony: they reflect the mentality of those who conceived them. In being perpetuated, many had been purified, and even if the method of the neoplatonists, which consisted of giving them a symbolic meaning, is vain, the poet can nevertheless make use of those fables, incarnating new thoughts within them, and making legend a vehicle that can bring minds the ideas of tomorrow."

The philosopher was suddenly interrupted by a great tumult. In the midst of a group of diners, two men were insulting one another and gesticulating. One of them, replete and robust, with an apoplectic face disfigured by wrath, was wearing a horse-dealer's blouse over a short jacket; the other, small and thin, with a jaundiced, tanned face bristling with a dirty graying beard, was clad in a faded charcoal-gray costume and coiffed in a frayed and stained white felt hat. He was yelping rather than screeching, while his adversary, rendered voiceless by fury, was impotent to respond to the insults heaped upon him.

The spectators were watching the scene complacently, and their satisfaction appeared to increase sensibly when the little man seized his enemy by the throat, which had the initial result of turning the already crimson tint of his complexion purple. As the fat horse-dealer, almost paralyzed by rage, was not defending himself against his aggressor, the indignant Marcus launched himself into the middle of the circle formed by the witnesses and, to their great chagrin, he separated the two combatants violently; their respective friends immediately surrounded them.

As for Juste, he had contemplated the spectacle with the most complete indifference, and it was in a mocking tone that he congratulated the philosopher for his philanthropic intervention.

"Why are you jeering?" asked the latter.

"Heaven forbid that I'm jeering," said Juste. "On the contrary, I admire your courage, but you might have employed it better. For myself, it would have been agreeable for me to see the man you helped strangled."

"Explain the reason for that ferocious humor to me."

"Willingly. This admirable inn, although it attracts gastronomes careless of luxury and appearances, is also the rendezvous of the usurers of Geronta and the surrounding area. It is here that peasants come to borrow on their crop, to put in pawn their cow or their plow, to eat their unripe wheat or their immature grapes, but those transactions, very useful to our agricultural prosperity, are not always untroubled. The little man you spared from future remorse is surely a wretched vine-grower, and the horse-dealer you protected is one of the best-known, richest and most avid moneylenders. I've known him for a long time; he's a client worthy of your benevolence."

"My friend, if, in suppressing that fat man your poor devil had suppressed usury, and, in consequence, that society that engenders it, you would see me inconsolable at having prevented his action, but the disappearance of that individual would not have changed the order of things, and it is a vile thing to see someone strangled."

As Marcus finished speaking, the waitress approached him and said that the individual he had obligingly assisted was requesting that he do him the honor of taking a glass of old wine with him.

"Gladly," Juste hastened to respond; and he said to the philosopher, in a low voice: "These people always drink the best vintages, and it's as much as one can get from them. Anyway, while I help them empty the bottle, you can doubtless converse profitably with them."

Marcus did not make any objection, and, following Juste, who was impelled by his ardor for drink, he came to sit down at the moneylenders' table. The horse-dealer shook his hand effusively, and muttered a few words of thanks, pointing at one of the guests, to whom the philosopher's gaze turned. He was an aged man of respectable appearance, who seemed to be the doyen of the company. He was clad in a black frock-coat and trousers; a golden chain over a white waistcoat emphasized the comfortable prominence of the abdomen and his clean-shaven face, with a florid and fresh complexion, had an expression of jovial tranquility.

He greeted Marcus with a gracious nod of the head and addressed him in these terms: "Our friend is inexpert in the oratory art; please excuse him if he has not been able to express his gratitude to you appropriately. He owes you a great deal, however; you have saved him from apoplexy, at the least. It might appear surprising to you that we, his colleagues and even his comrades, left the care of defending him to you, but that is quite natural; our intervention would have increased the assailant's rage and might have incited the indifferent to attack us, for we are not liked."

"Why?" asked the philosopher.

"Because we are usurers. That word surprises you, and perhaps you are astonished by the lack of art that I put into veiling the profession that we exercise. The term is, I know, commonly held in bad odor. That is, in my opinion, a prejudice against which we ought to protest, and is not the best way of doing so to take possession of a title that has been made into an insult?

"For thirty years, Monsieur, I have put all my efforts into restoring professional dignity among us, and my first action was to inscribe on my door, beneath my name, not 'business agent' or 'mortgage arranger' or, for instance 'credit administrator for all,' but 'usurer,' and that in capital letters."

"That is bold," said Marcus.

"A mediocre boldness, Monsieur. Does my neighbor not inscribe on the panels of his shop 'grocer' or 'baker'? What are we, if not merchants of money? Don't protest," he added, addressing Juste, who had, in fact, no thought of engaging in debate and had only opened his mouth better to admire the wine that the horse-dealer had just poured into his glass, "don't protest; you are about to fall into Aristotelian sophism and say, like the Stagyrite, that the nature of money is to be sterile. What an error, and what an unfortunate error! For the fathers of the Church, who were perhaps great saints, but particularly bad economists, have adopted the opinion of Aristotle, and that is the source of the misfortunes of our corporation."

Those words revived the rancor and the anger of the horse-dealer. He became crimson again and extended his fist toward the door through which his adversary had gone. Juste, mellowed by the Johannisberg, calmed him paternally, engaging him to forget in wine the memory of offences.

The respectable man continued: "Is it not the cry of hypocrisy that the universal protest utters against usury? Does not the merchant who comes to find me and borrows money from my coffers at thirty or forty per cent, which is the highest rate I demand, make a profit of fifty and sometimes a hundred per cent on the products that he sells? And it is often a single day's interest that that enormous profit represents. The merchant, however, is esteemed, but he scorns me; he will not give his daughter to my son in marriage. Why is that? Because we are the victims of the law. Is that law not iniquitous, and does it not violate the liberty of the citizens whom it prevents from acting in accordance with their will?"

"A great economist has thought like you, Monsieur," said Marcus. "Has he not written: *Every man of competent age and sound judgment ought to have the right to make, in order to obtain money, whatever agreement he believes, in his own estimation, to be advantageous to his interests?* And he added: *There is no more evil in extracting all the possible profit from one's money than in making any other advantageous bargain.*"

"Those are the very words of the illustrious Bentham!" cried the respectable man, enthusiastically. "In writing his *Defense of Usury*[1] he has written our breviary. For some years I've been preparing a critical and popular edition of that admirable work, and I intend to distribute numerous copies of it in the cities and the countryside, which will infallibly contribute to reforming opinion. Permit me to ask you, who knows my master so well, what you think of that mode of propaganda."

"It is excellent," the philosopher replied, and added, with a slight irony that only Juste understood: "If similar ideas had been propagated among the people a long time ago, the friends of Lumkine would not have seen what they have seen."

"Who is Lumkine?" asked the entire company, with a single voice.

"One of your brethren; would you like me to tell you his story?"

"Indeed," they exclaimed.

And Marcus began.

---

1 Jeremy Bentham's *Defence of Usury* was published in 1787. French Anarchists were, in general, not fond of Utilitarianism.

III

Lumkine

THE LIFE of Lumkine offers no particular distinction. It cannot be presented as an example, nor related in the practical manuals of morality in which one sees virtue recompensed in good gold coin or title deeds, and vice punished by the most abominable miseries. It was an essentially vulgar life. Lumkine, like the majority of men, was not an individual all of a piece, absolutely good or absolutely bad.

It is, in any case, a mediocre conception that allows individuals to be represented in a single shade, acting by virtue of a unique principle, moved by a sole passion or inspired by a sole desire. Even among those heroes whom history or legend shows us preoccupied by an exclusive goal and absorbed by a jealous idea, one notices a thousand contradictory sentiments, by virtue of which one can judge them differently.

That was true of Lumkine. One woman, at least, cherished him as the incarnation of devotion and tenderness. Lumkine had taken her in when she was scarcely articulate and had brought her up. For her, he was benevolence, and as she nourished a few old beggar-women, for those old beggar-women, who had very simple ideas, Lumkine was benevolence.

A traveler curious about mores and customs who, in passing through the village, had interrogated the rickety, the blind and the crippled individuals camped round Lumkine's house, would certainly have saluted him thereafter as a beneficent, mild and charitable philanthropist. He would not have been mistaken, but he would only have seen one aspect of Lumkine, for Lumkine was a scoundrel.

His rascality, however, was not such that it struck with horror all those who were witness to it or who heard descriptions of its features. Lumkine had never killed anyone. Although he had caused the death of many of his fellows, and had led many others to despair, he had never supposed that, by acting in his customary fashion, he was bringing about such irremediable misfortunes.

Unconsciously, he was an excellent economist, of a perfect orthodoxy. He knew all the profit that could be obtained from an item of merchandise, and in what fashion, by scrupulously following the law of supply and demand, the basis of civilized society, one could obtain the maximum benefit therefrom. But the only merchandise Lumkine had was the rarest and most precious: gold. He had had that gold at birth; it was a stock that the foresight of his ancestors had left him, and the only advice that his father had bequeathed him was to be a good merchant of that gold.

Many generations ago, his ancestors had rid themselves of the theological prejudice that weighed upon lending money at interest. At birth, Lumkine had learned that gold is a commodity, a commodity that is bought and sold, having its own value, like the cabbages and beets that peasants take to market, a commodity of which one can and ought to take advantage. He had never understood the anathemas by which the merchant selling his gold is afflicted, while sparing the industrialist who sells the iron manufactured by his workers. He had always thought that ostracism unmerited.

To be sure, he did not have enough scorn and horror for the men who gave carved stones or lots of straw hats to those who come to their native lands in quest of money; he sold gold, but loyally and honestly, never deceiving anyone as to the weight. He was the most upright of businessmen, but as his establishment was a good one, he sold dear.

The village where Lumkine lived was, like all villages, inhabited by a few rich proprietors and a large number of poor wretches, petty farmers who could never pay their rent, pitiful peasants who could never buy the seeds with which to sow their fields. All those poor folk were Lumkine's clients. He liked them a great deal and had more consideration for them than the rich; the rich had no need of him and did not enable his commerce to progress, whereas for all those starvelings, he was an indispensable man. When the rent was due, when the time for sowing drew near, it was necessary to go to the merchant of gold, and Lumkine's establishment was never empty.

Lumkine was detested by all his clients, because he was a scrupulous man, a man of honor. He was faithful to his word and he always fulfilled his engagements, which is how an honest businessman is recognized. He had never given a peasant a fake gold coin, and that was a virtue, because he could have done so without the borrower daring to protest. But he demanded from others the same regularity that he practiced.

As I have said, without ever having learned political economics, he could have given pointers to the masters of that science. With them, he affirmed that no one was obliged to come to him in order to have money, which was perfectly true, and all the needy people that came to him could have decided to die immediately rather than seeking by all possible means to prolong their pitiful lives. Thus, he said that his debtors had freely concluded bargains with him, and he did not tolerate any failure in their engagements. He was an upright man, a just man, and Lumkine knew how to use all the laws to oblige his fellow citizens to remain honest. He had their furniture and clothes sold in order to spare them the pangs that their conscience would certainly have suffered.

Lumkine's debtors, who were ignorant of the inevitable laws of political economics, hated the usurer ferociously. They were mediocre intelligences, but Lumkine was indulgent; he forgave them for the hostile sentiments that they professed toward him, and continued to lend to them at the useful moment. In any case, he lived for many years without the hatred of his compatriots being manifest in any other way than insults muttered as that misunderstood individual passed by. One day, however, Lumkine died.

The woman he had cherished as his daughter was in despair, and the old beggar-women wept for him, but all those he had obliged, all those whose creditor he had consented to be, manifested a frantic joy on learning of the disappearance of the philanthropist, and some of them were heard to say that they would be able to avenge themselves on the man who had held them to ransom. They did indeed avenge themselves, in a symbolic and terrible fashion.

Lumkine's corpse, set on a bier, was exposed in accordance with custom, outside the door of his house, and, during the night preceding the funeral, the beggar-women kept a vigil around it. In the morning, the guardians, having fallen sleep, were awakened by a frightful tumult. They looked around and saw that dogs were fighting around the cadaver; they uttered screams, and Lumkine's friends who came running saw that minced meat had been spread over the coffin, and the oak smeared with grease. The rude and vindictive peasants had wanted the man who had been, for them, like a tenacious and voracious dog, to have an escort worthy of him.

The dogs could not be chased away, nor could they prevent other meat from being thrown, especially by women, and Lumkine was conducted to the grave by a howling pack, whose clamors were accompanied by the laughter of a delirious crowd.

"Monsieur," said the respectable man, coldly, when the philosopher had concluded his tale, "I confess that it would be indifferent for me, personally, to suffer such a fate. Whether dogs or men fight around my coffin is unimportant to me. I do not know what you are trying to prove by your apologue, but its perfidy would have been pernicious for us if you had related it elsewhere. I believed, on hearing you cite Bentham a little while ago, that I might find a useful auxiliary in you. You have disappointed me, and I can see that you are similar to all our detractors, nourished by the same prejudices and imbued with an identical sentimentality. I will not make you any reproach, but I do not think that I will annoy you by affirming that our relationship will be ephemeral."

"I regret it," said Juste, "for the wine that is served to you here is excellent. But the bottles are empty and, since the Old Master began his story, my neighbor the horse-dealer has not ordered new ones. I see no inconvenience, therefore, in retiring, inasmuch as I have promised to show my friend the beauties of Geronta, and, thus far . . ."

Marcus stopped him with a gesture and a smile; he saluted the moneylenders, none of who saluted him, and then, followed by Juste, he left the hall.

IV

The Tavern of Hermes

AS they left the Inn of the Dove, Juste, while still on the threshold, uttered a profound and sad sigh.

"You're sighing like the Knight of the Doleful Countenance," Marcus said to him. "May one know the cause of your melancholy?"

"Is it not necessary to bid farewell, to this house, alas? Have we not gravely offended the worthy men who are its most faithful and its most considered clients?"

"Do you think, then, that in order to please those honorable money-merchants, the hotelier will banish us from his hostelry?"

"No, but he'll do worse. He'll serve us the scraps of the kitchen to eat, he'll give us an infamous verjuice to drink that he'll doubtless send someone to seek in a nearby tavern, for such beverages don't dishonor his cellars, and even the waitress will no longer acknowledge me. That is where virtue leads."

"You have only yourself to blame, Juste. If you had not jeered at my chivalry when I saved your friend the horse-dealer from the hands of his debtor, perhaps I would have limited myself to listening to the speeches of those who invited us to their table."

"You'd have acted sagely, but, since I've known you, I've observed that the nature of your intelligence always takes you to extremes. To save a usurer from death was excessively generous; to wound the sensibility of benevolent hosts who were fêting us so generously by way of compensation was unnecessary."

"Should I apologize to them?"

"Refrain from doing so, Old Master; fortunately, my ill-humor has already passed and I still know a few good corners. In any case, the speech of the man in the white waistcoat amused me greatly, and the effect produced by your anecdote was better than its consequences. I'll even make you a confession that might surprise you. I didn't find that our usurer was illogical in what he said. He's no more blameworthy, in fact, than the merchant who obtains an excessive profit from his merchandise."

"Would you like to tell me at what limit a profit ceases to be legitimate and becomes excessive? For our moneylender, as you heard, the merchant who sells his merchandise at double the price of purchase is a thief, and he considers that in lending at forty per cent he makes an honest profit. Others in their turn treat him as he treats the merchant, and so on. Is it not the opinion of everyone, moreover, that all profit is illicit—a sincere opinion, insofar as no one wants to speak of any but his neighbor's profit?

"In complaining about the ostracism that afflicts his corporation, the disciple of Bentham is right. Shylock is no less estimable than the industrialist who makes a fortune at the expense of others' labor; he just has a different fashion of making other's sweat productive. Why does one cry out against Shylock? Because our society needs pariahs, who are always useful, in order to establish official morality and give citizens the illusion of being virtuous."

"Since you think that, Marcus, why did you tell our hosts the story of Lumkine?"

"Have I told you that I hold moneylenders in esteem? The essential thing for me is to show every individual the value of his sophisms, to magnify, if necessary, the consequences of his actions, if I find them contrary to my conception of justice. For that, the apologue is excellent. It is part of my method, I make use of it as Plato made use of myths, because it renders ideas, doctrines, and even critiques and opinions, tangible."

"You have an answer for everything. Let's go together, then, to tell fables to the inhabitants of the city—for that's the reason, isn't it, that you have come to Geronta, as the apostle of a new era? If you wish, I shall be, not your disciple, I am not worthy of that, but your companion, and perhaps I'll be able to mingle my parables with yours. Don't say no," he added, precipitately.

Marcus took his hand affectionately, and they both set forth again.

All day they wandered through the streets, the crossroads and the squares of Geronta, and the philosopher admired the splendors of the city sadly, because he had brushed poverty in going through the outlying districts, which were only animated at that hour by the noise of factories in which an entire population of serfs was lamenting.

How meek people have become, he thought, *and how accustomed they are to slavery. One still finds them vulgar, and they certainly are, but how much resignation is enchained to their brutality! If, among savage tribes, a few people wanted to attribute to themselves the produce of the common hunt, the others would surely suppress them, either by cunning or by force. Here, millions of individuals support hunger and dolor,*

He thought that as he walked, and did not speak to
his companion, who refrained from troubling his reverie.
Sometimes, however, Juste pointed out to him some famous monument, an ancient edifice, a statue of a poet or
warrior, or an allegorical figure commemorating remarkable events or legendary heroisms.

Toward evening, the walkers found themselves on the
bank of the river that separated the two main quarters of
Geronta, that of the rich and that of the poor, for the city
was Carthaginian and did not admit any divisions other
than those—capital so far as its people were concerned—
formed by opulence and deprivation. The rich quarter
covered the sides of three hills, on which there was the
charm, the luxury and beauty of its villas and its park,
proudly dominating the city of the poor, whose narrow
and swarming streets plunged into the plain of black soil,
like snakes in mud.

In the middle of the vast river was a large island. An avenue traversed it; on one side a garden extended enclosed
by gilded railings; on the other stood a palace of archaic
style, flanked by towers reflected in the muddy water. Two
bridges linked the island to the two banks; they were closed
at their extremities by bronze gates, and that was the only
link that connected the city of the masters and that of the
slaves together.

Juste and Marcus paused opposite that island. On the
river, which the setting sun dappled with little sparkling
waves, the philosopher gazed at the boats that were set-

ting forth from huge warehouses, bringing the plutocrats back to their dwellings. Behind the line of the docks, in the submissive country, rose barracks, as if to protect that neutral territory, the source of Geronta's fortune.

In the dusk, the sound of clarions resounded, to which the distant appeal of a siren responded. The powerful and nostalgic odor of tar mingled with the perfume of spices and Oriental wood, and sometimes, the breath of spring passed over the water; it came from the gardens of the rich and brought the aroma of hawthorn and syringas. It seemed to Marcus that all those balms had to stop at the white walls of the barracks, and never refresh with their breath the sad suburbs, the rumor of which he could hear increasing.

An immense sadness invaded his being; he felt his heart wrung by a redoubtable anguish; his eyelids lowered, and for a second he had the sensation of being dragged away by the waves that were fleeing before him. But his weakness did not last long, and when he opened his eyes again, the towers blackened by time struck his gaze again. With a gesture, he indicated them to Juste, and Juste said to him: "The Palace of Justice."

"Let's go," said Marcus.

They crossed the bridge, at the entrance of which were placed bad allegories of Justice and the Law; they went along the avenue bordered by restaurants and cafes frequented by advocates and clerks of the court, and, after having gazed at the façade of the redoubtable edifice momentarily, they went into the interior courtyard. It was the time when the courtrooms were closing, and the crowd was invading the corridor and the vestibules, descending the steps of monumental staircases and hurrying toward the doors, separating there into two streams, of which the larger and more tumultuous headed toward the plain.

"What miseries and what iniquities is that torrent carrying away with it?" Marcus murmured. "For what satisfactions have all those people come in search here? Perhaps the rich have reassured their fear at the sight of the law that always strikes, and the poor have forgotten their woes at the spectacle of the misfortunes of others. Dread, cowardice, vile curiosity, the base love of vengeance, cruelty and abject cupidity are the guides of all those fleeing people. Could one alone be found among them who had come to this horrible temple to exalt his love of truth and justice?"

He might perhaps have continued for a long time, but Juste drew him toward one of the corners of the courtyard, where a vaulted gallery opened, preceded by a landing from which it was separated by a low door.

"Let's go in," said Juste, "and take care to give a few coins to the man standing on the threshold."

They went in, and after having accomplished the indicated ceremony, the philosopher was introduced into the vault.

"Who is that Cerberus to whom we paid tribute?" he asked.

"He is the most avid of the inhabitants of this palace. He accumulates the most malevolent functions. He is the intermediary between the Treasury and the condemned, between the advocates and the magistrates, between the prisoners and those who cherish them. He does evil in three forms and knows how to extract a profit from all of them. At the end of this gallery is the interior staircase that leads to the prisons. You've seen what it's necessary to do in order to be admitted to see those who will shortly be brought down here; it's necessary to submit to the same ritual if one wants to speak to them or procure them some kindness.

"His second mission is more delicate. The judges of Geronta are the most upright of judges. They are unapproachable, and their door is closed to solicitors. But our man's door is always open, he is always ready to listen, ready to receive, and the magistrates' door stands ajar for him; he is the messenger that the purest receive and to whom the most incorruptible listen.

"Nevertheless, he is not only the spokesman for delinquents and advocates; he is the agent of the receivers of fines, and that is where he can show all his ingenuity. Not content with receiving a large salary from the members of that redoubtable corporation, he levies his tithe on the jugs of wine he distributes with the sole aim of obtaining from the various tribunals sentences profitable to his patrons. He does more; as he is the clerk who records those fines, he knows how to falsify the sentences cleverly in ordered to impose a tax on the collectors who have already paid him. Thus he merits the name of Torturer-by-Pen that was given to him by a poet overcharged by him."[1]

"That poet was literate," Marcus observed, "and he had read Philo, who mentions in one of his opuscules a certain Lampo, a prefect's clerk, a great enemy of Jews whom the people of Alexandria called Calamosphacte, of which Pen-

---

1 "Plume-Bourreau" [Torturer-by-Pen] is, as Marcus says, a French translation of *Calamosphacte*, a term allegedly coined by Philo of Alexandria, a Hellenistic Jewish philosopher of the first century B.C. in a diatribe against one Flaccus. A French translation of Philo's works appeared in 1870, which Lazare had evidently read; the word does not appear in Charles Yonge's English translation and the attribution of the diatribe to Philo is dubious.

Torturer is the translation. But this is not the place to talk about Philo."

As he was speaking they had arrived at the extremity of the gallery, which was closed by a thick grille, behind which the last steps of a stairway ended. Into that narrow space a hundred people were crammed. Juste indicated them to the philosopher.

"They're the wives, mothers and friends of those condemned today," he explained. "They're going to be taken back to their cells now, and those whose tenderness remains faithful to them come to console them, to give them a smile, a tear, or the shadow of a kiss. Many years ago I went down those steps, but no one was waiting for me in the passage and solitude was my only companion. Pardon me for having brought you with me to make this pilgrimage. I wanted to salute those who are my brethren, the only ones I love and for whom my heart can stir, those whom life has struck and whom the ferocious machine up above has finished crushing. Look at them now."

The lamentable procession had just appeared; chained in pairs, the convicts were moving under the conduct of guards and, once again, before disappearing into the jail, they were able to regret the free life in seeing their relatives. Sobs, appeals, stifled cries and plaints were audible, which rose up from the midst of the watchers, in the midst of whom the last to arrive were striving hopelessly to reach the grille. Among them, a woman impotent to cross the living rampart begged in vain to be allowed to get closer. Juste seized her and lifted her up above the crowd; she extended her arms and uttered a cry, a name, and then pulled free and turned to Juste.

"Thank you," she said. "Without you, I wouldn't have been able to see him."

"What has he done?" asked the philosopher.

"He refused the salary offered and struck the master, alas. What folly carried him away? Couldn't he bow his head?"

"What are you saying?" exclaimed Marcus. "Isn't bending the spine and bowing before injustice the evil that engenders all evils?"

"Shut up," Juste begged, as the frightened woman fled. "Those aren't words that ought to be pronounced here. You're going to criticize my cowardice, I know, but I once felt the claws of the cat digging into my shoulders, and I wouldn't want to be subjected to it again. If you interrogate the people surrounding us, you'll see the same fear in their eyes that convulsed the eyes of that woman just now, and the same fear would make their hearts beat faster if a word of revolt emerged from your lips."

"Let's go, then," said Marcus; and, preceded by his guide, he quit the somber gallery. As on their arrival, the redoubtable Pen-Torturer saluted them as they left. They found themselves back in the courtyard, now deserted, and left the Palace, the metal doors of which were being closed.

"If you wish," Juste proposed, "when they were on the avenue, before night falls we can go to rest for a moment in the Tavern of Hermes. There, no doubt, we'll hear a few jovial remarks. In any case, the fresh air has returned my good humor and I observe that it's a long time since I had a drink."

"What a fortunate man you are, Juste! You have a soul of sand, whose dolors are effaced under the wings of the evening breeze, and you're almost an optimist. But what am I saying? Your eyebrows are frowning and your expression is darkening; I forgot that it's time for you to drink. Tell me, then, as we walk, what the place is to which you're taking me."

"It's a place renowned throughout Geronta. One finds all wines there, all the beverages in the world, from the most archaic nectars to the most modern liqueurs. If you drank, you'd be able to be served hydromel, cervoise and perhaps even ambrosia; you'd be given sack and huff-cap, like Shakespeare's companions, falernian like the guests of Lucullus and Pteleatic wine like the friends of Theocritus.[1] I drank those when I was young, in the time when I was trying to dissipate my guardian's thousand francs; today I've recovered from such romantic follies, good for students on the spree and the idle, and I limit myself, when I can escape the water of public fountains, to a few old and authentic regional vintages.

"That is not, however, what ought to attract you to the Tavern of Hermes; that establishment, the rendezvous in the evening of idlers and night-birds, is the place where the quibblers and clerks of the court gather. Advocates fraternize there with businessmen, ushers and shady agents; they traffic placidly with the honor of folk, conspire against their fortune, tax the innocent and impose customs duties on duties that ought to be defended. It's there, in sum, that the prologues are written to some of

____

1 *Cervoise* is a hypothetical ancestor of beer. *Trousse-chapeau* [Huff-cap] is taken from a French translation of speeches by Pistol in a scene in Henry IV Part I, in which Prince Hal is drinking with Falstaff and his companions, but it does not seem in the original to refer to a kind of beverage, and the English term is the popular name of a kind of mushroom; Pistol appears to be using it metaphorically to refer to boasting. Ptelea, the supposed place of origin of a wine mentioned in the idylls of Theocritus, is on the island of Cos.

the plays of which we've just seen the denouement, and of all those that conclude in misery, despair and the shameful death of those who are the unfortunate protagonists. But here we are, outside the antechamber of Themis; let's go into the lair of those subtle jurists."

The main hall of the Tavern of Hermes was beginning to empty out when Marcus and Juste made their entrance, so they were able to find room at a corner of a table without too much difficulty, and while Juste—who, in spite of what he said, liked to vary his drinks—ordered port wine, the philosopher examined his neighbors.

"Listen to what they're saying," Juste murmured in his ear. "The clean-shaven man with the cunning face who is speaking is the most celebrated advocate in Geronta. He has the glory of having defended all the financiers who are sent before the judges from time to time, when they permit themselves to bite into the cake of the rich and aren't content the shear the flock that's abandoned to them. He's never accepted to help an innocent man, and it's him who made a celebrated quip to the son of a poor man who came to solicit him on his father's behalf, and to whom he refused his aid: 'Innocence, Monsieur, is its own defense.'"

Marcus listened to the clean-shaven man. He had a resounding and unctuous voice, but very nuanced and full of charm, a voice at times hypnotic, susceptible of drawing an adversary into judicial nets, dissimulating them not by means of the flowers of rhetoric but by the envelopment of reasoning that was simultaneously captious, logical and sophistical. He was talking to a neophyte, and everyone fell silent in order to listen to the celebrated rhetor.

"Our profession, young man," he declared, "is the most elevated and the most ancient in the word. It goes back to the divine Word, pleading before God to defend the posterity of Adam, more unfortunate than culpable. That Word is our eternal and miraculous patron; it is also our inspiration; it indicates our goal—which is to say, the goal to which the law tends. We must be the heralds and the knights of the law, if I might put it thus; it is important that, at every minute of our life, we remember that we have, not a profession, but a mission to fulfill. What other men call extraordinary qualities, advocates consider as indispensable duties, and their heart must be the hearth of all generous sentiments."

A long murmur of approval welcomed the orator's words. Juste appeared to share the general admiration and he drew nearer to the group that surrounded the master. The latter continued: "What noble sentiments tradition has left us, moreover! It is not content to teach us that probity, toil and disinterest are our divinities; it sustains us with its counsel in all circumstances. Behold the precious and touching heritage, a common heritage that no one in our corporation can deflect to his unique advantage. Is it not the voice of the ancestors the recommends us only to accept a case after having examined it with the most scrupulous attention, and to defend it only if it appears just to us? Is it not that voice which enjoins us not to impose excessive honoraria on fear, or to the embarrassment of people, and to moderate exaggeration if their alarm brings them to us? It is that which enjoins us, above all, to be the soldiers of right."

At that point, Juste thought he ought to shed a tear of tenderness and amazement, and Marcus one for his hypocrisy. The clean-shaven man seemed touched, and continued, this time addressing himself to his sensitive admirer.

"Such is the sublime beauty of our function. So what more admirable title is there than ours? To be defenders, to snatch human beings from the rigors of fatally inhumane laws, to fight against a judge whose breviary, the Code, must render him pitiless; to be the counterweights of social vindictiveness: that is our role, and it is thus that it is necessary to stand up before a magistrate, who is its representative, and who employs all means to satisfy it. Apart from a certain category of individuals belonging to the dangerous classes, whom it is important, for the common good, to leave at the free disposal of tribunals, we ought to oppose the cunning and legal and legitimate malice of the judge, always ready to punish those who have only used, in daily combat, their individual capabilities, and are simply the victors in a regular battle."

Juste's enthusiasm no longer knew any bounds, and the great advocate, interrupting his speech, addressed to him, on behalf of all those present who belonged to the bar, his thanks for the sympathy he was testifying to them—at which a skeptical listener made the remark that Juste might well be nothing but an adroit solicitor.

"You're mistaken, Monsieur," Juste replied. "I have not come to bring you any case. I am a vagabond and pauper by estate and more likely to be a judge's client than yours. That's why your master's speech has touched me. You give the impression of being too subtle a psychologist not to know that men are linked to one another by their common antipathies. I have a horror of magistrates and you are their adversaries; that is the secret of my affection for you."

"You doubtless have personal reasons," retorted the skeptic, "to justify such an animosity."

"That's possible," riposted Juste. "What saint can affirm that the original motive for his most ardent and most altruistic passions is not egotistical? At any rate, I consider judges as pernicious animals."

"He isn't wrong," affirmed a few voices in the crowd that had gathered to listen to the discussion. Juste recognized that his auxiliaries belonged to the clan of businessmen, direct enemies of Themis, fighting against her on the shifting terrain of the Code.

Glad to be thus supported, and caring little about the quality of his allies, Juste continued his diatribe. "They are the worst and least estimable of criminals, for they kill, ruin, despoil and torture without danger. Nero, who liked those games, at least merited, at the same time as the esteem of a few men of letters, the execration of posterity, but the man who disposes every day, at his whim, of the life and property of a few wretches, maintained by the representatives of force, enjoys common consideration. He is the master whom no one must touch. And every judge accepts such a responsibility without anxiety; he never has uncertainties, and I do not know of any, except those in a few legends, who have been assailed by remorse or by fear."

"What legends?" someone asked.

"Would you like me to tell you one that was told to me one evening, a long way from here, aboard a boat that was going downriver toward Cologne?"

And without waiting for a response, Juste spoke.

V

The Judge's Adventure

JUDGE ARNOLD had the custom, every summer, of going to repose near Bingen, on the bank of the Rhine, in a placid little hamlet where he forgot the cares of the magistracy. For two months he led a quiet and vegetative life here, pruning the rose-bushes in his garden, giving feed to his chickens and, during the hot hours of the day, reading collections of ancient fables, of which the eternal hero was the great river roaring at his feet. When evening came, he went to sit down under the arbor of a tavern that overlooked the water, and from which he could see the last houses of Bingen, the schloss that served the Bishop as a temporary refuge from vengeful rats, and, on the other side, on the summit of a hill, a brand new statue of Germania.

That was the best time of the day, the one in which the judge savored the silence of people and the murmur of things. He heard the splash of the waves dying on the banks, far from the tumult of the great flood heading toward the sea, and he became softly tender in thinking about the destiny of the drops of water that the spongy soil drank, and which would never see the steeples of Cologne after having reflected those of Mayence; for Judge Arnold was sentimental and if, during the year, he was able, by virtue of professional duty, to be insensitive to human dolors, during his vacation, he was exceedingly sensible to the sobbing of forests and the plaint of waves.

That summer, on the eve of his departure. Judge Arnold was sitting under the arbor in his habitual spot, drinking little sips of the brown beer that was served to him every day, and which was brewed in the hamlet itself: a tasty and fresh beer that he only drank there and regretted all winter. He was lost in a melancholy dream, only emerging from his reverie to drink, surrendering himself to the heady charm of the beloved beverage; one tankard succeeded another, and he listened to the rumor of the river.

All evening, joyfully laden boats had been going downstream, carrying bands of musicians and singers toward Bingen, who were going to celebrate some musical festival, and refrains intoned by sonorous voices had troubled the peace of the hills and the banks.

When midnight came, silence had reconquered the village, and Arnold, before going back to his garden and his house, decided to go for a stroll along the bank of the Rhine. He stood up, his head feeling a trifle heavy, and, although his eyelids were fluttering, slightly troubled by the fumes of the beer, he went downriver at a slow pace. The night was very dark; he thought that the moon, which was already blue-tinting the heights, would facilitate his return, and he marched resolutely.

He went blindly, pausing to look at the brilliant dots that were dancing before him, while denser shadows succeeded them and seemed to be accompanying his march. He was not astonished by that; his soul was familiar with the people of the air and the spirits of the waters. He knew the names of all the children of the Rhine, and he would not have been surprised to hear himself called by some gnome, a guardian of treasure or a tormentor of peasants. He knew the words that captivate them and only feared the malign and perverse nymphs of the river.

The ground, becoming softer, and yielding somewhat beneath his feet, told him that he was getting closer. He could hear the nocturnal song of the waves more distinctly; it was more intense, more dolorous than during the day, when the sun made emeralds and opals sparkle on the crests of the waves; night weighed the waters down, muffling their impact, and in the profound bed there was something akin to the endless uncoiling of a velvet serpent, the curves of which might have been brushing soft walls.

A slight splash alerted the judge; his foot bumped into a hard object. He bent down and groped around; his hands encountered a tree trunk raised on a heap of stones, doubtless in order to serve as a bench. He sat down there and, as his eyes adapted to the obscurity, he contemplated the old Rhine, whose foam was flowing processionally.

He felt very happy; a great peace invaded him. He told himself that nowhere, not even enclosed in his study in Leipzig or beside his flowering rose-bushes, could he savor such a delicious quietude. His nostrils dilated in order better to breathe in the moist perfumes of moss and the scent of the water, the slightly limp but penetrating and evocative scent extracted from the thousand shores whose trees had bathed their branches in the current, and whose earth had been eroded by the Rhine, drawing with it the resinous odors of wood and rural fragrances.

Arnold thought he saw passing before him, reflected by the mobile and fleeting mirror, the objects that had leaned over the river to be captured and retain there, of which its inconstancy had only kept the image prisoner in the crystal of its gaze. He saw the profiles of cities, distant profiles that seemed to hide when he leaned over in order to distinguish them more clearly; and then flat quivering meadows, with the sound of cow-bells, and clumps of trees animated by the fluttering of large birds. He would have liked to seize them all at the same time: the trees, the meadows and the cities; an intense desire gripped him to depart, to go a long way from the hamlet, and even the tavern where he drank such good beer.

He extended his arms in front of him, stood up, and moved even closer to the river, listening to a distant rhythm of oars: those of a boat for which he was waiting, which he divined, and which was coming; a long boat guided by a silent rower.

It stopped in front of him; the rower made a sign. With an indescribable joy, Arnold stepped aboard and let himself down onto the poop bench, with his back to the tiller, stretching out his legs and tilting his head back, while the boat went slowly down the Rhine. A sense of wellbeing invaded him; he let his hands dangle over the sides, and the fleeing water caressed his fingers. It coiled around him like little snakes that milk from bowls might have warmed up, and sometimes rose along his arms, forming warm liquid bracelets, the contact of which made the judge feel faint.

He closed his eyes and had the sensation of gliding endlessly: a profound, seductive sensation of infinite softness, by which his entire being was penetrated and possessed. He became part of the great peaceful river, his body dissolved in its fraternal waves, and it was not only on his hands that he received the caresses of the flow. Enlacements surrounded all of his flesh; serpentine forms rose up around his legs and embraced his breast; soon he felt supple rings pressing his throat and neck, and it was finally on the mouth that he received a prolonged, insinuating and tender kiss.

He divined that a lorelei was drawing him away and he felt recklessly happy, because he had dreamed of that adventure for a long time, of going to live under the crystal vaults with the undines, whom he cherished. So he did not resist, and did not even want to raise his eyelids, waiting to touch the bed of the Rhine in order to gaze at the individual conducting him.

Now he heard a thousand sounds emerging from the waves, and as if he had acquired a new sense, he understood the plaint of the drops of water, the song of the foam, the rumor of the fluvial host; he was amused by the laughter of the crowd that pressed around him. He was pushed maliciously, pleasantries were murmured in his ears, urgent appeals resounded, and everything melted into a monotonous swell, from which surged, from one minute to the next, a squeal, a snigger or a sob.

Arnold thought that he was about to reach the goal and tread the white, fine sand that was at the bottom of the river; he abandoned himself more flaccidly; the whole aroma of the water entered his nostrils; bells were ringing, swinging in invisible belfries, silvery at first, expanding in tense sounds whose vibrations ran over the judge's skin like thousands of sonorous insects, and then full of a tempest of bronze, beating Arnold's head with their powerful carillon and making his entire body quiver. They attenuated their fury; the voices of silver and the voices of bronze fused, uniting in a broad, voluptuous wave of harmony, the circles of which spread out, englobing within them the sounds that had animated the Rhine a little while ago, and then retracted, dying away in a prolonged, shrill, perforating melody; and silenced allowed its heavy mantle to fall over the waves, which were weighed down by it.

A dolorous anguish descended over the judge; a metal weight compressed his breast; mechanically, his hands tried to draw apart, but he perceived then that he was bound. The malign goddesses had wound rushes and weeds around his limbs, which resisted the efforts of his legs and arms. He tried to swell his muscles in order to rid himself of the burden that oppressed him; he could not do it. Under the burden that weighed him down he made great efforts, he summoned air, but his mouth was closed; his eyes were bloodshot; he could hear the impact of the blood beating in his veins and arteries and running in tumult beneath his skin, which was becoming tumefied.

Suddenly, he saw a large sheet of light; it appeared to him to emerge from his pupils, to extend over the river and vivify it again; the harmonies that the waves had kept captive sprang forth again, subtler, more refined and more seductive. His anguish dissipated; he felt the bonds that held him loosening, the heavy armor that enclosed him splitting; he heard it crack, descending along his sides, and he heard the sound of his fall into the Rhine.

He was able to open his eyes; he breathed in forcefully; the tide that was surging in his blood-vessels eased; he had reconquered calm and forgotten thought when an unexpected turbulence seized him. He was carried away with a vertiginous rapidity, in a damp and fresh breath, toward unknown depths; and abruptly, a violent collision arrested him.

He was in the boat, still lying near the poop, and the vessel was going downstream. The moon had risen; its light was paling the sky and descending over the hills, awakening the grape-clusters and causing the leaves to shiver; it glided over the thickets neighboring the banks, cleaving silver valleys in the somber masses, and mingling its bright waves in a thousand nacreous streams with the majestic waves of the river, which were impregnated with light at that contact.

The waters were twisted in white swirls; swans seemed to be playing in the eddies: swans and women. Arnold saw their necks and their arms extending toward the boat that was carrying him, and he was leaning out to seize them when the boatman, letting go of his oars, touched him on the shoulder, stopping his impulse, frightening the birds and the nymphs, which disappeared.

At that unexpected contact the judge sensed his fear take hold of him again. Something drew him down to the river bed, holding his arms captive with the thread of the water, and at the same time, the boatman's hand fixed him to his bench. He forgot the swans, the nymphs and the beautiful silver flowers decorating the waves, which the soft breeze coiffed with a filigree of foam; he could no longer hear the mocking laughter and malicious comments of the children of the Rhine; he listened to the silence that weighed upon the clear mirror of the waves, on the bank and on the hills; slowly, he was impregnated with terror, without any cause, for the river had been his friend and he no longer feared its ill will.

Silent and motionless, he looked at the companion whose fingers were digging into his flesh. He was a very tall man clad in a long dark cape. Arnold could not see anything of his face but his eyes, eyes of an imperious magnetism that were shining intensely. He tried to look away but he could not, for he suddenly understood that the boatman was about to speak, and he reconquered his tranquility, ready, as an old professional, to undo the ruses of an interrogation that he supposed would be knavish and fallacious; but the placid honesty of his interlocutor defied his expectation.

"Don't you think," said the other, "that the time has come for me to know you. You have asked me for hospitality; I have given it to you, and have taken you for an excursion on the old Rhine; but it would please me not to have entertained someone unknown."

"What!" Arnold replied. "You impel your boat over the river near Bingen and you don't know me? Don't you know that my name is Arnold?"

"I didn't know that," replied the boatman, "for I'm not an inhabitant of these banks where you're popular. I'm glad to know your name."

He meditated momentarily; then he let go of the judge's shoulder, sat down again and, picking up the oars, he directed the progress of the boat.

Clouds had invaded the sky, hiding the moon; a thick darkness extended over the banks. Little blue phosphorescences were dancing on the waves, sometimes racing toward the boat. Arnold sensed their luminous effluvia caressing his fingers; he heard their soft sizzling, which mingled with the duller slashing of the water. Again he divined around him the troop of undines and naiads, and again the voice of the boatman, almost invisible, so dense was the night, awoke him from the dream to which he was abandoning himself.

"What are you among men?" the strange individual asked.

"I'm a judge," said Arnold.

"A judge?" queried the boatman. "What's that? Do you mean that you measure the actions of your neighbor, that you are able to place them in the true balance and that you don't falsify their weight?"

"If you wish," Arnold agreed.

"A judge," repeated the boatman. "You're a judge! Does that mean that you sound hearts equitably, that you know the motives of all actions, that for you, the most obscure crannies of thought, the darkest intersections of brains and souls, are illuminated?"

"You credit me with too great a power," said Arnold, smiling at the admirable candor of the savage.

The judge's response appeared to surprise the boatman profoundly; he quit the oars and meditated deeply, while the judge, amused by that naïve questioning, evoked his courtroom in Leipzig. He lent an ear to the response of an imaginary accused, whose face he saw, not without delight, tortured by anxiety, and he began to laugh: a slightly bitter laughter, which seemed to fall into the water like rain, and to play in the midst of little vagabond flames, some of which bit Arnold's hand more sharply. He shuddered, and fell silent.

"So," said the boatman, "you judge men?"

"Yes," said Arnold, becoming impatient with that insistence.

"Explain to me how."

Arnold shrugged his shoulders, but a secret instinct warned him not to indispose the person who was questioning him, and, with a benevolent condescension he told him how, on certain days, clad in a special robe, coiffed in a determined bonnet and sitting in an elevated armchair, he examined the conduct of a few poor devils that guards brought before him.

"What have those men done?" asked the boatman.

"They're criminals," Arnold declared.

"What do you mean by that?" asked the boatman.

"I mean that they've committed reprehensible actions."

"Hmm! What do you call reprehensible actions?"

"Those that are reproved by the law."

"And these men that are brought to your tribunal, you know them, no doubt?"

"Why do you think I know them, when I'm seeing them for the first time?"

"Then you don't know their life, and what circumstances presided over their birth? You don't know if destiny has been mild or terrible to them? Their joys and their dolors are unknown to you? You have not learned who their educators and guides were; their ancestors have not been named to you and you have not been told what they were and when they engendered the man whom you have summoned between your soldiers?"

"I don't know any of that."

"You have, then, a divinatory sense, you are, or you recognize yourself as, a superior being, missionary and anointed, to whom all weakness and all error are foreign? You are inflexible, just, honest, beyond reproach, fearless and devoid of hesitation? Let me admire you then."

The boatman bowed to the judge, who experienced a malaise, and could not support that humility, which seemed to him to be ironic.

"Don't admire me," he said, with bonhomie. "I'm a man like others."

"Then why," said the boatman, "do you judge your brethren?"

"Because I know the law."

"You know the law?"

"Yes, while young I was taught to know the meticulous net; I was shown its mesh—mesh that paternal authority tightens every day. I know all those who attempt to escape its grip, those who can pass through its intersecting threads, and also those who cannot."

"That is what you call judging, then?"

"That's what it is."

"And you've never had any remorse? You've never doubted your ignorance or your presumption?"

"Are you joking?"

"Certainly not! And you would see without fear, coming before you now, those you have judged in your life?"

Arnold hesitated momentarily, and then, in a very low voice, he said: "Yes."

Then the boatman stood up and said: "Come with me; you'll doubtless be pleased to confront them."

He extended a finger. The judge saw that the boat had run aground on an island that he had never seen in the river. A strange frisson shook him. He felt an unknown fear, and suddenly, the boatman, having seized him, lifted him from his bench and threw him on to the unknown terrain.

It was a bare and deserted shore, the sands of which extended infinitely. Arnold wanted to ask his guide what that mysterious country was, but, having turned round, he saw that he was alone, while in the distance, on the river, the individual who had brought him was drawing away.

His legs were heavy, and yet an irresistible desire to march impelled him. For a moment, he sat down on a rock, which seemed to soften under his weight; he could not stay there, for an indistinct, toneless voice spoke in his ear:

"Come."

He got up and set forth, straight ahead, like a deer free of the hunter and returning to its shelter. His lassitude had become indifferent to him. He expected something and, anxious to know what it was, he hastened his steps. The strand along which he was moving seemed limitless; the expanses of its sands were prolonged, and he was surprised suddenly to see on the horizon the violet mist that the respiration of trees causes. The wind brought him the cherished perfume of resins, the powerful and beneficent sylvan odor; then he heard a rumor softer and sadder than the rude clamor of the river: the nocturnal murmur of dormant woods, stirred by dreams.

He traversed a region of gorse and brushwood, studded here and there with clumps of stunted pines; and, like a somber portico, the forest opened up before him. As he penetrated beneath its foliage, he stopped, because he had heard footsteps. A shadow was coming toward him along a path; it was his companion. He told himself that perhaps he had brought the boat to some haven, and was not astonished to see him again.

"Come," said the boatman. "They're waiting for you."

The judge put his hand in the man's hand, and allowed himself to be drawn along the path. The night was so profound that he could not see the features of the person guiding him. Around him he heard the rapid and panting breath of people running; he thought that he was in the midst of a horde. He closed his eyes while walking, and tried to count the soldiers of that army, but he could not do it, only perceiving a confused cadence, and he was becoming impatient when he heard the boatman say to him: "We've arrived."

The judge looked. He was in a vast clearing, in the middle of which there was a platform surrounded by a silent crowd. On the platform, an old man was sitting; a man was standing before him. Arnold understood that the man was about to be judged. A great curiosity took possession of him. He wanted to know how magistrates proceeded in this strange country. He went forward; the crowded parted to let him pass, and he was soon in the front rank, opposite the accused, whose face he could not see.

"What has he done?" he asked.

"By his fault, creatures similar to him have perished," someone beside him replied.

"Why isn't he made to perish?" he asked.

"You're prompt," said an ironic voice in his ear. "Do you know how and why he made them perish."

"What does it matter?" Arnold replied.

He was about to continue when the old man made a gesture and shouted in the silence: "Let the accusers approach."

Someone emerged from the crowd of people and climbed the steps of the platform. His face was known to Arnold; doubtless he had been in contact with him before, and, as he was clad in wretched rags, he thought, being a good judge, that the plaintiff had once been one of those on whom he had passed judgment.

"You accuse him?" said the old man.

"I accuse him," replied the man. "I once had a field and I lived on that field, but the moneylender also lived on it, and a time came when he alone could live on it. One evening, I struck the moneylender, who had come in search of his ransom, and I took from his sack a portion of what he had extracted from my sweat and my distress. This man condemned me."

"I remember that," exclaimed Arnold, and then began to laugh, because, although he had once judged a similar crime, it was not him who was in the dock at present. Perhaps, he thought, it was a prevaricator or criminal judge who had been summoned, and he was on the point of saying that such unworthy testimony ought not to be admitted, but the man continued.

"I was imprisoned for a year. When I was released, my field was someone else's field and my roof was no longer my roof. Since then I have lived without shelter, without a hearth and without bread, harassed by everyone, as stray dogs or the beasts of the woods are harassed, and I shall die like them, in a ditch or on the edge of a pond, or struck down one evening, as my sister was struck down, whom he also condemned, as my mother was struck down, who was subjected to his judgment, as my brothers have been struck down, and all those who were punished for having suffered, all those he has tortured, all those he has killed, all those who surround him."

On hearing those words, the crowd rushed toward the platform, and pressed around the accuser, and the man who was being judged cried: "I have accomplished my task; I have done my duty; I have served the law."

"He's right," said Arnold. "I have done likewise; we are not responsible for the wounds that the blind sword of the law inflicts."

With those words, the man standing on the platform disappeared, and Arnold saw that it was himself who had just been accused; he recognized the man who had spoken and he also recognized those who were beside him: all the rogues, all the poor devils, all the vagabonds that he had punished because they were hungry and thirsty, because they had eaten their neighbor's bread and drunk someone else's wine, because, weary of the rude and solitary roads, they had wanted to know a soft and warm bed where one could sleep.

He recoiled before them, and the grave voice of the old man pronounced the sentence: "I deliver to you the one who has always applied the law and has never known justice."

Then, like a pack of dogs, the crowd rushed upon the judge, and the judge fled through the bushes into the tenebrous forest. He ran without respite, pursued by the vengeful mob, stumbling between the hostile trees, held back by enemy brambles, all the way to the liberating river, whose waves called to him, and welcomed him, when he delivered himself to them, like a child going to sleep in a woman's bosom, in order not to hear the terrible echo that was repeating: "Judge Arnold has not known Justice."

VI

Dialogue

"IS that the conclusion?" asked the clean-shaven man.

"If you wish," Juste replied, "but if it doesn't satisfy you, I can tell you that a week after that night, Arnold was found a few leagues from Bingen. He was lying in the reeds of the shore, where the current had cast him up. It was on that tragic end that the legend was embroidered, and from the naïve popular imagination the tale emerged of the judge pursued by the avenging Erinyes, tormented by the scorpions of remorse, and escaping them by means of death."

"It's very improbable," observed the skeptical listener.

"You're right," Juste replied, "and I've always thought, personally, that the honest man was drowned, having got drunk."

A burst of laughter greeted the storyteller's riposte—approving and satisfied laughter, for the members of the audience could admit, without being shocked, and even with a malign satisfaction, the drunkenness of a magistrate.

"Does that story seem good to you, Old Master?" Juste asked Marcus, when the hilarity had died down.

"It appears mediocre to me," replied the philosopher, toward whom gazes turned. "Not that its form was disagreeable, but the ideas that it tries to express are incomplete. Your boatman is intelligent enough, but he doesn't get to the bottom of things; he has a superficial mind, which has good tendencies, but he lacks logic and isn't capable of following an argument through. As for your judge, he's endowed with a truly wretched brain, unable to find either an excuse for his actions or to give an explanation of them. It's evidently simple minds who imagined that myth, which they doubtless only required to satisfy their rancor, and not to bring them a superior ethic."

"You must know a more perfect story, Marcus, and also more profound. Don't be miserly with it, for I don't know any place more propitious than this one for speaking about Justice."

"About Justice, indeed, Juste. That's what my subject ought to be, and if these gentlemen will permit. I shall tell my tale in my turn."

"We're ready to listen to you," said the illustrious rhetor, amenably. "Only permit us to fill our glasses again, and that of your companion—for, if I've observed correctly, you abstain from alcoholic beverages."

Marcus inclined his head, and when everyone had drunk, he started speaking.

VII

The Administrator of Justice

ON the day when Queen Berthe learned that her judges were selling justice, she was gripped by a frightful sadness. She was a woman with a tender soul and a sensitive heart, even capable of suffering the pain of others. The late king, her husband, having been a whimsical and sanguinary despot, a ferocious and brutal master, she had resolved, after his death, to consecrate her existence to the wellbeing of her subjects and to enable them to forget the bad years that they had endured. So, when she was informed of the iniquity of her magistrates, she was in despair. She thought of all those whom those measurers with false weights had mistreated, and she suffered in thinking that she had aided in spreading evil. However, she had dressed in ermine and purple men of proven virtue, austere old men, and younger enemies of vice whose benevolence ought to have tempered the rudeness of rigid elders. All of them had failed in their mission; they had allowed themselves to be bought by the rich, had scorned the plaints of the poor, and had helped in the despoiling of the wretched.

On listening to the story of their misdeeds, Queen Berthe sobbed, as she had done in the morning when the life of the late king had been revealed to her. She tore out her blonde hair, because she was heartbroken at the thought of those despoiled and persecuted innocents, and her despair was poignant, because she understood that she would never again believe in the goodness or the honesty of judges.

From then on, she resolved to be the administrator of justice, the redresser of wrongs, the infallible dispenser of recompenses and punishments. Her realm was not large; she could be sufficient to the task that she was imposing on herself. She went through the valleys and over the mountains, listened to the groans of the poor and the sobs of the humble; she was mild toward the sad individuals whom the powerful held under the yoke, and hard on those, whoever they might be, who attacked the property of others.

One morning, she arrived in a village that she had never penetrated before. It was in the depths of a solitary valley, surrounded by a green circle of high mountains, in a landscape of tranquil and opulent gaiety. When one descended by the winding road snaking down the mountainside, the houses of the village looked like islets in the midst of a yellow ocean of wheat, in which the wind hollowed out supple and undulating ripples. Queen Berthe did not neglect to admire that spectacle, and rejoiced in her heart at the thought that, in this corner of her realm, everyone must know wellbeing and joy.

All the villagers came to meet her; they wanted her to sit down on a litter embellished by woven ears of wheat. She consented to that, and they carried her in that fashion to the square in front of the church, where an oak armchair covered with white fleeces was standing. There, young women approached, carrying fine baskets of wheat pancakes and fruits, and earthenware pitchers of perfumed milk and warm, sweet wine.

Queen Berthe accepted the collation that was offered to her, and then mounted the rustic seat. A herald, after three blasts of the trumpet that the echoes of the valley repeated, invited those who had grievances and complaints to come forward and approach their sovereign.

Many of them came forward, and spoke in their turn. They were all men and women with florid complexions, vigorous and proud in their mannerisms, clad in rich and plush fabrics. They came before the queen, competing for the steps, complaining of minor reciprocal usurpations, and their voices had a frightful hardness when they said "my field," or "my wheat."

The good Berthe attempted to conciliate the mutual interests of all those tenacious peasants. She consoled herself for their very visible harshness by thinking that none of them had committed a crime or an evil action, and she was about to retire when she perceived a man fraying a passage who was shoving before him an unfortunate tatterdemalion, thin and pale, whom everyone was greeting with insults and blows. When they were in front of the royal tribunal, the men-at-arms seized them and separated them, and the queen asked what crime the person who was being thus maltreated had committed.

At that request, a frightful clamor went up in the crowd; everyone ran toward the administrator of justice and started shouting. The man who was being dragged to her throne had lived for years on theft and rapine. He lived in the depths of a remote gorge, in a solitary cottage from which he emerged at night in order to steal chickens or the milk from cows. He set his snares between the furrows, he levied a tithe on the fruits of orchards, and the man whose arms had finally seized him had caught him in the process of reaping in his own field.

"Why do you take the property of others?" the Queen asked him, severely. "Don't you know that it is written that *thou shalt not steal*?"

The poor devil looked at the woman who was speaking to him; he opened his mouth to reply but, having cast a glance over the mob surrounding him, he shrugged his shoulders and remained silent; Queen Berthe could not obtain a response from him, or any defense. She could see clearly that he was obstinate in wrongdoing, and thought that it was necessary to punish him. She exhorted him once again to respond, but, her objurgations having been vain, she sentenced the guilty man to three months of severe imprisonment. Then, as no one else presented themselves, she ended the audience and, after resting for a few hours, she left.

Three months later, as she was returning to her capital, the Queen passed through the valley again. It was evening. As she came down the mountain-side, she heard confused clamors rising up, cries of menace, anger, rage and despair, and, on arriving at a small plateau overlooking the village, she saw in the distance a howling mob pursuing a semi-naked man who was bounding through the hayricks.

The mob drew closer and in the last rays of the sunset, Bethe distinguished the gleam of scythes, mattocks and axes that the pursuers were brandishing. The fugitive was, however, gaining ground, and would doubtless have escaped his enemies, when he suddenly stopped. He had just perceived the royal cortege. He seemed to have a momentary hesitation; then, resuming his course, he climbed the slopes of the mountain, with the furious troop still on his heels. Closely pressed, on the point of being overtaken, he stumbled and fell under the feet of the horses, while the soldiers held back the frantic mob.

The Queen recognized the pursued man; it was the thief she had sentenced previously. She gave the order for him to be picked up, for he was exhausted by fatigue. She interrogated the assailants, in order to discover what new misdeed the wretch had committed, but the vociferations were such that no one could hear her voice.

She was about to repeat her question when someone behind her said: "You want to know what that man's crime is? It's to have submitted to your justice."

Berthe turned round. She saw a herdsman of vulgar nature, with a hirsute and graying beard and skin wrinkled by the sun and the rain. Somewhat disdainfully she said: "Explain yourself, fellow."

"Willingly, Queen. Listen to me. That man, thanks to you, was thrown in prison, and for three months he had to wear a carcan. Now, yesterday evening, when his jailers released him, he fled like a wounded wolf, and out there, in his hut, he found his wife and child dead of starvation, no one having given them alms or a crust of bread. Then, fury seized the unfortunate, and when morning came, he killed the man whose brutal hand had dragged him before the tribunal. That is why the others are pursuing him; that is why they want to demand his death."

Bitter sobs swelled Queen Berthe's breast. An immense despair took possession of her, and she murmured, very softly: "I haven't rendered justice, then!"

Quietly as she had spoken, the herdsman had heard her.

"No one can render justice," he replied, "except to himself, and you most of all, Queen, do not have the right to be an administrator of justice, since you contribute to perpetuating evil."

"Me?" she said.

"Yes, you. Isn't it you who defend those who possess? Are you not the protector of those who surround you, those who own the vines and the fields, those for whom the poor are the eternal enemy? You rejoice in the prosperity of this land, but while rejoicing in it, you do not think that all that wealth only profits a few. When someone was brought to you whose only crime was to have wanted to live, you punished him, saying that it was necessary not to have taken the property of another; you did not have a word to ask how that vagabond had been welcomed in this valley of abundance. You struck him because he had eaten, and your justice ought to be satisfied, since it has caused the death of three human beings."

Queen Berthe bowed her head; her tears flowed more abundantly; she recognized the vanity and impotence of her justice, since she had exercised it in favor of the unjust; she also understood that as long as there were poor and rich, what was called justice could never be anything but defense: iniquitous, cruel and futile defense. She thought that her power maintained that which was evil. Then, having dismounted, she embraced the man whose body was shivering in the cold of the evening, and quietly begged his pardon, while the old shepherd shook his head.

❋

Several times, while Marcus was speaking, murmurs had become audible. When he fell silent, the anger and indignation of the lords of chicanery were given free rein; they expressed their sentiments in a violent and insulting fashion, which showed how the daily practice of affairs had exasperated their combativeness. For a few minutes, nothing could be heard in the tavern but offensive and wounding exclamations, to which Juste did his best to respond, in spite of the fact that they were not aimed at him.

"He's attacking order," said the clean-shaven man, eventually.

"He's misjudging justice," cried the skeptical listener.

"He's a dangerous man," added the former.

"Abominable," someone shouted, "odious and infamous; the most redoubtable of sycophants, the most pernicious of sophists."

"He's threatening public peace," someone affirmed.

"He's sowing revolt," added another.

"It's necessary to deliver him to the police," proposed the great orator, "and put him in the hands of the judges; he can relate his parables to them."

The philosopher remained impassive; he listened to the invective and the insults, smiling, and it would have been easy to believe that they were not addressed to him, but rather to Juste, whose anger was increasing with the rage of the assailants. Perhaps excited by the wine, he did not spare his adversaries, calling them hypocrites, cutpurses, robbers, sworn tormentors, liars and catamites. As he could not make them shut up—and, on the contrary, the clamor was augmenting—he showed them his fist and challenged them.

That was a bad move, for the young clerks, less hardened and always ready to pass from words to deeds, suddenly hurled themselves on him and his companion, to the applause of the skeptic and the illustrious rhetor. Juste received the first blows that were rudely delivered; Marcus attempted to defend himself with his cane, but he would surely have succumbed under the weight of numbers if someone had not thrown himself between the combatants, striving to calm them down.

"Go through the kitchen door," that unexpected defender said to the two travelers, "and wait for me at the entrance to the bridge to the low city. While you flee, I'll calm the fury of these fanatics."

Juste and Marcus, understanding that they could not have the advantage against such a strong troop, followed their protector's advice. Not without taking a few punches, they succeeded in freeing themselves and, and protected by the waiters, whose sympathy they had gained, they succeeded in crossing the threshold of the unfortunate tavern.

VIII

Conversation on the River Bank

"IT would be prudent to forget our dignity," said Juste, simply, when they were out of the reach of their aggressors, "and flee as quickly as possible. One is very stupid when one has been drinking; I've just given proof of that by playing the knight errant, and I should have imitated your example. Let's take advantage of reason having returned to me by respiring the air of the river, and let's go without delay to wait for our new friend at the arranged rendezvous. We can leave him without scruples, for he appears to know the regulars of that accursed place; anyway he hasn't offended them as we have done, and he'll be able to soothe their bellicose humor."

Marcus made no reply. Motionless, with his back to a tree trunk, he was meditating, and perhaps had not been listening to what Juste was saying. He must have been evoking similar scenes, and a bitter sorrow creased his brow; he reviewed the stages of a long pilgrimage, mentally marking the stations of his life as a propagandist. Before his half-closed eyes extended the route already traveled; he saw it extended to infinity, always as rude and as painful, and he wondered whether it might not be better to lie down there, on the road. With what delight he would have rested his weary body, his exhausted legs, and how good it would have been to forget them in sleep and in death!

Mechanically, he stuck out his chest, advancing his lips as if toward a cup; soft and soporific waves descended from his brain toward his limbs, and he abandoned himself to being invaded and conquered by them.

Juste's voice woke him up suddenly.

"Don't be so dejected, Old Master. What do you expect? It's our destiny to be abused and maltreated. A few months ago, it was valets and farm dogs that were my persecutors. Thanks to you, my life has changed, and those inferior torturers have been replaced by usurers and quibblers, while waiting for better ones. But since we've escaped miraculously from the blows of those bag-carriers, let's be joyful, and above all let's not start another brawl by virtue of our provocative presence. Shall I confess it to you? For all the times I've been beaten up, I haven't yet got a taste for it. Anyway, if we stay here, we'll miss out on having a word with the generous stranger who helped us."

"You're right," said Marcus. "It's necessary to forgive my weakness if my shoulders droop occasionally under the burdens with which my youth charged me, after some combat and if, when soporific night comes, I weaken in thinking about the formidable task. That, I believe, is a residue of ancient vanity. Once, drunk on hope and universal love, I set forth one morning thinking that I was a new Messiah treading the soil of the path, and that at my summons the dormant earth, developed like a mummy in the bandages of its egotism, its indifference and its pride, would rise up: a chimera of demigods, elect men, founders of sects, initiators of religions and reformers nursing utopias; a beautiful dream, that only satisfies a few noble minds and candid and ardent children.

"No voice is powerful enough to awaken the world; we are no longer in the era, if there ever was one, in which walls fell at the sound of trumpets. The old décor that seduces and frightens human souls is rooted too profoundly in the soil to be able to crumble under the blows of a lone individual. Let our effort be humbler! It's slowly that new shelters are constructed. The task of wanderers like me is to recruit the workmen of the new endeavor, to prepare hearts for a better existence, to create more perfect consciences, to give birth to just desires and possible hopes.

"When the beautiful gardens flourish in which humanity can stroll with liberty acquired, the fortunate city will surge from the soil of the ancient city and, under the rush of the joyful crowd, the age-old walls of oppression will buckle as the battens of a door buckle under the blows of a battering-ram. But none of us will see that day of delight; we are similar to the obscure quarrymen who extract blocks of marble and will never know the marvelous edifice whose construction they will permit."

While he was speaking, they arrived at the entrance to the bridge, where their defender was to join them. There was a stone bench in the middle of a clump of poplars. Marcus sat down there and Juste remained standing before him, ready to announce the advent of the man for whom they were waiting.

The philosopher fell silent again, and for a moment his companion refrained from interrupting his mutism. He contemplated the old man affectionately, and meditated on what he had just heard. His meditations could not be of long duration, however. He was an excellent debater, alert and prompt to riposte, but his mind, accustomed, like him, to vagabondage, was unable to constrain itself to reflection and incapable of holding on to a thought, so the most various sensations, images, impressions and ideas passed without consequence over the mirror of his consciousness, and he hardly cared about giving an appearance of reason to their succession.

That mobility, in fact, made him the most amiable of companions, and Marcus cherished him for his insouciance and his naïve love of material satisfactions, which equaled his indifference to poverty. He often listened to his rambling; it was restful for him to listen to the other, and only the latter's silence could surprise him. He was already astonished when Juste, weary of his role as lookout, came to sit beside him.

"I was busy looking for the jovial side of our adventure, and haven't found it. We've been insulted and beaten, and except for having forgotten to pay for what I drank, I don't see what advantages we could have obtained from that visit to the Tavern of Hermes. On the contrary, it's another place that is henceforth closed to us, and I'm obliged to console myself for that by giving myself all sorts of excellent reasons. In any case, whatever I said, I detest the clients; they bring with them an odor of stacks of paper and cells that's very unpleasant. I even fear that they aren't really the enemies of the magistracy, and that brings me to the point I'm trying to get to: can you tell me why that mob listened to me benevolently, and why it welcomed the story of Queen Berthe so poorly?"

"The reason is simple, my friend, and you ought to have understood it yourself. In relating Arnold's adventure to those men and concluding it as you did, you flattered some of their opinions, if not their passions. Doesn't a fiction, sanctioned by the law and by custom, oppose the defender of individual interest to the representative of the collective interest of the privileged: the advocate to the magistrate? You did nothing else, before them, but maltreat the conventional adversary, the rival brother, a guardian like them of the established order; you were the satirist of a corporation against which they battle, while remaining on the same terrain, and you amused them, in the same way that, by changing your hero, you would have amused a tribunal.

"But those orators, those men of affairs, if they combat judges, live on the Law, the traditional Law, and it's the Code that also furnishes them with their weapons. They willingly make such plays on words as Torturer-by-Pen, and will applaud yours, but they refrain from suppressing him; they will laugh at the prosecutor who accepts bribes, but they conserve him carefully and seek him out. They act like the good Christians of old who teased monks, cardinals and priests while joyfully surrounding the pyres on which heretics were burned.

"You're a fault-finder, but I'm a heretic. I struck the divinity itself, and not the servants of the divinity; I blasphemed the idol that nourishes its faithful, and the herd whose provender I threatened rushed upon me. I didn't, moreover, find the anger of those men abnormal; their chagrin, their irritation and even their violence seem natural to me."

"Because you're full of forbearance," proffered a young and grave voice from the shadows.

Marcus and Juste looked round, and saw someone standing behind them. They recognized him.

"Thank you for helping us," said Marcus.

"My bones owe it to you that they aren't broken," said Juste in his turn. "Accept the testimony of their gratitude."

"You don't owe me anything," replied the unknown, "And it's perhaps for me to solicit your indulgence. Since the moment you came out of the Inn of the Dove I haven't quit you. I followed you, listening to your discourse, and I've been marching on your heels all day, lending an ear to your words. I was by your side in the suburbs and the city of business; I paused with you by the river, went into the Palace of Justice with you and accompanied you to the Tavern of Hermes. Master"—as he said that, he bowed to Marcus—"would you like me as a pupil?"

"What is your name?" asked the philosopher.

"Claude."

"You ought not to have any master but yourself, Claude. I'm only a man who knocks at the door of souls, who calls out in the darkness. In this city of pride and despair, you are the first to have heard me; be very welcome and let's work together on the open road. As you sustained me just now, I'll sustain you. Who are you, Claude?"

"Until today, I was a poor seeker of the unknown. I was born among those who possess; I've lived, I've thought and I've suffered. I've known the hopes of mornings, faded as soon as they opened, and the mortal despairs of dusks; I've gone to sleep in impotence without having attempted effort. I won't tell you the incidents of my life; they're vain, as it has been vain, and what would you want to know about me except for the thirst for action that devours me? Your voice has awakened me; it has shown me the beacon in the night, don't ask me for anything else; let me follow you and sow fallow human ground with you."

"Let's go together, Claude; I cherish you already. For love of me, I beg you to love Juste. If you've heard him, you know him. He's a precious companion; he does not know doubt; his practical philosophy can shore up your uncertainties, and his optimism will cheer you up. You're frowning? Claude, refrain from the cult of suffering. Do your dolors seem to you to be at the likeable point at which you want to conserve them? The heavier your task is, the lighter your soul ought to be; divine joy is the strength of heroes, and bleak silence cannot be uncreative. Don't say, as some do, that it's necessary to bear the misery of the world and weep the tears of others; it's not sympathetic sobs that people need; leave the tears to weary elders and show a joyful face to those toward whom you go."

"Well, then," said Claude, "let Juste lend me his support."

"Gladly," Juste replied, "But before anything else, I'll ask you for yours and beg you to guide us to some hostelry. The Old Master will tell you that I worry about my stomach; he's not wrong, and I think, with reason, that I've neglected it for too long. It would be bad for me to continue, and I only have a distant memory of this morning's meal."

"It's necessary to satisfy Juste's desires," said Marcus.

"We won't leave the island, then," Claude declared. "Since it's necessary to satisfy our friend's impatience and hunger as quickly as possible, I know a suitable place nearby, solitary enough for our dinner not to be troubled."

The two men approved that proposal, and, having abandoned the clump of poplars, they followed their guide.

IX

Irène

WHEN they quit the modest inn to which Claude had taken them, night had enveloped the Palace and the confused mass of trees shading the garden, into which they had not yet penetrated. Only the avenue was illuminated, by powerful electric reflectors, and it rose toward the hills, on the sides of which sparkled the frontons of theaters and circuses, and the chandeliers of places of pleasure. A bitter scent descended the slopes, mingled with the perfumes of spring, scattering over the river: a subtle and irritating scent made of the artificial balm of incense, the vapor of feasts and the odor of lust.

In the other direction, the somber buildings of the docks and barracks seemed to be crouched on the ground, some like animals ruminating, others like surly and attentive dogs. Beyond them plunged the boulevards and streets, the tangle of which was designed by the rows of gas-lamps bordering them. On the horizon, a circle of fire enclosed the city, consisting of ardent factories. From the island one could see the large bay windows of rotundas reddening, and gigantic chimneys plumed with igneous vapors. Thanks to the distance and the darkness, nothing could be seen of the furnaces but the tall brick chimneys which were rearing up like flamboyant tripods burning before invisible statues of gods; and they were indeed formidable and terrible gods whose worship they announced. Thick fumes escaped from their craters, traversed by crimson flashes, fogs that were simultaneously fuliginous and white, obscure ruddy glimmers, violet-tinted plumes, green incandescences and long yellow flames dominating all the rest. Over the black houses accumulated around the furnaces, stars of scoria and sparks fell, and an enormous tawny cloud that eddies of light agitated incessantly floated above them.

Marcus was leaning on the parapet gazing at the blazing horizon. With a gesture, he indicated it to his companions.

"At that spectacle, have you never experienced the vertigo of tomorrow?" he asked. "What obscure consciences are those making the future! There, in the workshops, where it is not only iron that is being forged, a universe is in preparation. The slaves who are moaning under those vaults are agitating like blind moles and advancing toward a goal that is unknown to them. They satisfy needs, and thus create others, which, in their turn, give rise to others. The desires of the poor are born of the insatiable luxury of the rich, and the force of those desires will smash the world one day.

"But my brothers, sowers of dreams and revolt, from what ocean of blood and tempests will the new lands emerge? You're shivering, Claude; can you feel the cruel anguish of the first initiations? Were you not born of a rip and a bloody wound? Be the intrepid servant of justice, and don't preoccupy yourself with the laws that govern childbirths. Who can tell, in any case, whether the work that we're announcing might not be accomplished in the calm of a beautiful evening, an evening of forgiveness and forbearance, the breeze of which will appease rancors and soothe angers and hatred, an evening of wellbeing and tranquil peace, similar to the chimerical evening of the Messianists, when the fawn and the tiger will graze side by side, after the benevolent racket of theophanies. What do you think, Juste?"

"When that hour comes, Old Master. I'll have forgotten for a very long time the aroma of wine and the odor of meat, so I'll have arrived at the same point as you, who scorn them. It seems to me, in consequence, unnecessary to include that preoccupation in the order of my everyday thoughts. I have, it's true, a special philosophy. I attach myself to the present moment, I suffer from it or I enjoy it, for I'm a passive being, and if I were less idle I'd seek to embellish it, but without thinking about what my neighbors' grandchildren will see.

"I certainly don't offer myself as an example; even so, I can't see the advantage that you can obtain from these pseudo-prophetic speculations; as they're fatally uncertain, they can only trouble minds and arrest your propaganda. It's necessary not to show people too large a meadow to be mown, but, on the contrary, to enclose them in a little vineyard with a fence, where they can do good work. It's crazy to think about tomorrow's task when every day brings sufficient trouble of its own. What are you trying to do? Fray for others the path that you think is good, the one that ought to lead them toward justice and the good. Don't require them, however, to ask how you'll get to the end when you've scarcely started out."

"You're always right, Juste," replied Marcus. "Didn't I say, Claude, that this good companion was the fount of wisdom? One might find his boldness facile, for it doesn't weigh motives or ideas, but it doesn't matter, because an excellent rule for practical and active life can be extracted from his speech. Follow his advice; it will give you the delight of the free peasant, whom every dawn finds in his field, resuming the work of the day before, and who only looks up when a nearby cloud obscures the sky above him. Sow, my friend; under a bright sky or a stormy sky, the wheat will ripen one day; isn't the essential thing that the crop is planted? For us"—his hand indicated the black city ringed by flame—"the furrows are always ready. Let's go, Claude; guide us; it's time to descend into the plain."

It was late, a damp and glacial wind was coming from the river; shivering, Juste started running to warm himself up; Marcus and Claude followed him. At the exit from the bridge they went past a squadron of soldiers carrying lanterns, and Claude told them that continuous patrols went through the streets after sunset.

"Duty is thus inculcated in those men. During the day, when they're in their barracks, they hear talk of the salvation of the fatherland, whose guardians they are, and of neighboring realms whose ambition menaces the territory, but in the evening they're put in the presence of veritable enemies: the proletariat, still susceptible of anger, whose possible assault it's necessary to anticipate and the violent forms of demand. What an ingenious fiction is that of the foreign rival, the hereditary adversary! It helps to sustain our plutocrats; by virtue of it they succeed in mobilizing one part of the laboring class against the other, in such a way that, whatever the result of a civil war might be, only the wretches bearing the weight of it will suffer its effects. So all the efforts of moralists, philosophers and historians concur in fortifying that fiction and embellishing it; the schoolmaster spreads their doctrines so well that the poor really believe that they're protecting their hovels, which no one is threatening, and in receiving their daily ration, they defend their right to die of hunger."

The tremulous flames of the lanterns faded into the night, the cadence of footfalls died away, the confused shadows of the lantern-bearers disappeared and the three men resumed their march.

They went along a deserted boulevard, which cut at a right angle the broad street on to which innumerable stores, warehouses and cellars opened their doors, and then traversed a silent labyrinth of tangled streets, in the middle of which muddy gutters ferried detritus that, at intervals, rose up in monstrous masses. Low houses with sticky walls and narrow windows bordered each side of those stinking tunnels.

Already, at this hour, not yet late, no passers-by were animating the solitude of the abject quarter, but Marcus divined that an entire population was swarming there, and the cracked façades of the buildings seemed to swell under the pressure of the thousands of beings living behind them. He perceived a breath made of a thousand breaths, the heavy breath of a sleeping, harassed beast, worn out by fatigue; it passed through the disjointed plaster, the twisted planks, the worm-eaten beams; it came along cold corridors to poorly-fitted doors, and its rhythm animated the atmosphere floating above the viscous water. It brought with it the strong odor of sweating flesh, with which thousands of generations had impregnated the stones, the odor of those who toil incessantly from dawn, and whom the sledgehammer of a stupid sleep stretches out on their wretched beds in the evening.

Behind the walls, Marcus saw all those bodies lying like rags, faces swollen, chests sunken, backs arched and limbs disjointed: human machines only stopped by night. Unfortunate and profoundly exhausted, emptied of their strength and their marrow by the redoubtable and perpetual labor, they would have been unable to understand the philosopher, if entering their dwelling, he had touched their shoulder with his finger and announced to them the advent of the day of abundance: the day that nevertheless passed through their dreams sometimes, as it haunts the imaginations of the Indians who eat earth, the pale subjects of hunger.

On sensing those intelligences and those dead wills nearby, fear gripped the three companions, and even Juste found nothing to say. Involuntarily, they hastened their steps in order to get out of that prison camp and, after having passed its limits, they stopped for a moment, troubled and oppressed by the noise and brightness of a living street, a street of base debauchery where noisy drunken bands were emerging from the numerous taverns and the antechambers of the brothels that opened on either side of the sidewalk, vomiting violent alcoholic effluvia.

"The central street of the Pandemonium quarter," said Juste. "I must confess that I've frequented this crapulous place and know its corners, doubtless better than Claude. I've had all the vices, Old Master, and, even if your morality is scandalized by it, I don't regret it, having found satisfactions therein. My obligatory asceticism has refined my tastes, which is unfortunate, because it hasn't given me the means of contenting them, while rendering intolerable the vulgar jubilations of old. I truly believe that all the riff-raff of Geronta arranges to meet here; I have many friends among them, but I'd rather avoid encountering them; they don't interest me any more and they'd oblige me to drink atrocious liquids that my stomach can no longer tolerate. So, if you don't mind, we'll flee this crowd. Anyway, it's very late, I'm exhausted, and it's important to find shelter for the night."

"You think of everything, Juste," replied Marcus. "I confess that I hadn't thought of that, although my legs are weary; but I'm counting on you to indicate lodgings to me."

"Friends," Claude interjected, "accept my hospitality, I beg you. Why stay with strangers? Is my house not yours, is my roof not your roof? Juste is right, the night is wearing on; come with me, you'll be fed in the antique manner, a warm bath will refresh you, and you'll find supple and perfumed sheets on your bed."

"I've never had such a host," cried Juste, joyfully, "and I'm ready to accompany you anywhere. How about you?" he asked Marcus.

Marcus was about to reply, but Claude suddenly point-ed at a woman who had just brushed past them.

"Let's follow her," he said, simply.

She was a small and frail woman whose face disappeared beneath the hood of the large brown cape that enveloped her. As she turned her head Marcus glimpsed a young face with emphatic features, a fresh and fleshy mouth, a high forehead and large shining eyes. She was walking at a rapid pace and, strangely enough, as she passed by, the agitated crowd opened up, ceasing its obscene songs and laughter.

She stopped for a moment; a drunken old man had fallen down beside her. She bent down, wiped the mud-stained face of the recumbent man with a handkerchief, and then, at a sign from her, two men picked him up and carried him away.

"He's being taken to the nearby shelter," said Claude "One of those she's had built."

"Who is she?" the philosopher asked

"She's Irène the Visitor, the only daughter, now an orphan, of one of the most rapacious and powerful bankers in Geronta," Claude replied. "When her father died, having been a widower for many years, she abandoned her villa and came to live among the people. Of the gold that her family had amassed for centuries she only wanted to keep the fraction strictly necessary to maintain her life; she gives away the rest incessantly, without respite, carried away by the fever of pity and the horror of a fortune conquered from the misery of others, putting the same determination into despoiling herself that her ancestors put into enriching themselves. She lives in a small house by the riverside; she's only to be found there during her few hours of repose, for her unquiet ardor impels her to wander through the city, visiting the most sordid hovels and the most infamous dives, giving to each of those who are groaning the shadow of a joy and the appearance of a stroke of luck."

"Here she is," Juste interjected.

They had arrived at the entrance of the house of refuge, and Irène had just appeared on the threshold. Marcus advanced toward her.

"Would you care to receive me, Irène?" he asked. "For long months I've been walking, and the stones of the road have torn my heels. I'm old, as you see, incapable of any labor, and if I can't rest for a day, I won't be able to resume my route."

"Come in," said Irène. "Be welcome here."

Followed by Juste and Claude, the philosopher went into the vestibule. There, having sat him down, Irène washed his feet and wiped them gently; then she engaged him to eat something. She was getting up in order to lead him into the next room, when Marcus placed his hand on her arm, and begged her not to do anything else.

"Thank you for your benevolence," he said, "and perhaps I'll accept your offer in a little while. Before anything else, permit an old man to ask you a few questions." As she nodded her head, he went on: "Are you content with your work, Irène?"

She did not reply immediately; a shadow of hesitation dulled her gaze, but, rapidly, she stammered: "Why shouldn't I be content? I'm doing good."

"Does doing good consist of bandaging a few of the wounds of evil without curing them?"

"What do you mean? I don't understand what you're saying. Explain yourself."

"How troubled and impatient your soul is, Irène; already you're pressing me. Are you no longer so sure of your joy?" He fell silent, ad the resumed: "I'm accustomed to speaking in parables; if you would like to listen to me, I'll tell you the story of someone who was your sister. Her benevolent voice might perhaps show you the road along which you're marching."

"May you give me peace!" she murmured; and, supporting her head in her hands, she listened to the man whom the unknown had brought her.

X

The Error

IN that distant and perfumed land, everyone knew little Anne, and yet no one could have said where she came from. No one knew whose daughter she was, and yet they had always seen her there, since she was a little child, pretty and slightly wild, wandering the roads. She had grown, but not much. In the sunlight, while the good wind had tanned her skin lightly, as free as the birds of the fields, as placid and as modest as the flowers that grow in pathways. Only once, and for a few weeks, she had consented to work as a farm-girl, but she had left one morning without asking for her wages.

She was very strange, little Anne. Many people thought she was mad, and if they gave her the pieces of bread necessary to sustain her life, it was because they had a superstitious veneration for her. Some regarded her as one of the legendary saints who neither wove nor spun, any more than the lilies of the fields, and they admired her. As for those who, not knowing her, encountered Anne on the roads, they stopped to admire her because she was very beautiful.

She had large and profound tawny eyes, sunk in a
pale face, a forehead as narrow and pure as that of Greek
statues, a rather broad but marvelously-designed mouth,
minuscule ears and a straight and slender nose. Then, falling over her neck, spreading over her shoulders, caressing
her figure, was a forest of silky chestnut-brown hair, har-
moniously disordered. But what was seductive about her
face was not the rebellious curls of her hair, nor the lines
of her nose, nor her lips; it was her large eyes, profound
and tawny, because her eyes were moistened by ardent
pity, promising consolation; it was those eyes in which one
could contemplate the little soul of little Anne.

They did not lie, those eyes, and in life, Anne had always wanted to be a consoler. She had always had pity, a
puerile pity, sobbing if she were unable to liberate a fly
caught in a spider's web; and weeping just as much, but
not more, if she could not help someone who was injured
or wretched.

For a long time—a very long time—she was unhappy,
because she was not rich and it was forbidden to her to
give alms. When she saw some stout chatelaine distributing meager largesse, her heart melted in regrets and she
was devoured by envy, for she thought bitterly that she had
nothing to give. For a long time she was sad and morose
in thinking of her impotence; but at twenty years of age
she changed.

At that time, one evening in June, a passing vagabond
raped her on the edge of a wood. She put up little defense
against the attack and, without knowing what her assailant wanted of her, even showed a certain complaisance.
In spite of her frail appearance she was a robust young
woman and once the deed was accomplished she felt more

pleasure than regret. So, far from feeling anger against the rapist, she huddled against him and kissed him softly.

Then, instead of fleeing like a wolf, which is the custom of his peers when they are tracked, the vagrant, soothed by the caresses, told little Anne about all the joy that he had had in pressing against her flesh, and how good her lips had been to him. He told her then that one of his cruelest despairs was not finding, when he halted in the evening and the doors of farms were closed, and dogs were released in the courtyards, and servants armed themselves with their pitchforks, a tender female hand that would have taken his, made him sit down on an embankment and given him a little of the love that everyone refused him.

Having said that, the vagabond applied his lips once again to little Anne's forehead, and he left.

After that adventure, Anne remained thoughtful for a few days; she meditated. She thought that all those who wandered over the hills and plains were doubtless similar to the lover that she had had briefly, and that they would also welcome gladly the approach of a friend. As she thought about that, a great jubilation invaded her; she was happy, infinitely happy. Henceforth, she would no longer be poor, she would no longer envy anyone; she would have some-thing to give those who were suffering, and that something would be herself, the youth of her body, the softness of her mouth, the tender gaze of her eyes, the perfume of her hair and the enlacement of her arms.

From then on, little Anne was the consoler of vaga-bonds. She went to meet them near the woods that they had the habit of frequenting and she offered herself to them with the modesty of a bride. She learned, in order to say them to them, the soft words that bandage wounds, the words that are caresses in themselves, which put anguish to sleep and lull dolors. For the isolated and the refractory she was all of womanhood; she had the attentions of a mother, the concern of a sister and the transports of a lover.

She had never been as joyful. She was indifferent to the insults that disdained lovers hurled at her—for she always refused to abandon herself to the village youths who wanted her to add another pleasure to their pleasures. She was insensible to the scorn of young women, and did not experience any chagrin when the matrons who gave her daily bread out of devout dread called her foolish and fallen. She took the crust and went away, dreaming about the disinherited darling that she would doubtless see at dusk.

That lasted for years, and in spite of the profligacy of her life, little Anne was still as pretty, as slender and as modest; she still had the appearance of a wise virgin. Her face was a little thinner, though, and the expression in her eyes had changed; they were no longer moistened by pity, but illuminated by an apostolic ardor. Her happiness was still as great; however, it had to perish one day, as all happiness perishes.

One evening, an evening similar to the one on which she had encountered her initiator, near the same trees, she thought she saw him again. Her heart beat rapidly when she approached him and he looked at her very sadly. Like the first time, she huddled in his arms and told him about her life since he had had her. When she had finished, she offered him her mouth, but he did not take it, and she saw then that he was not her first lover. He contemplated her for some time and, having contemplated her, he spoke to her.

"You're mistaken, my darling," he said. "I don't say that you've done badly, but you're mistaken. Listen to me carefully and understand me. It's because you are being charitable in this fashion that you are making more tolerable the evil that ought no longer to be tolerated. Those who are committing the iniquities are relying on you to attenuate the rancor they provoke. Thus, your works engender wickedness. The necessity is not to soothe the distress of the unfortunate, but to prevent there being any unfortunates. The necessity is not to distribute largesse but justice, and you can, for your part, work for the reign of the justice that the world awaits. Leave this country, abandon those you believe that you are serving, and come with me to serve them better."

Having spoken, he stood up and offered his hand to little Anne. Little Anne stood up, all a-tremble. A great clarity illuminated her soul; she suddenly saw what egotistical joys she had satisfied. She did not hesitate; she cast a long glance over the familiar landscape, uttered a sob for the past, and, confidently grasping the hand of her guide, she departed with him into the clear night.

"Will you do the same, Irène?" the philosopher asked. He pointed at the windows, which were paling. "Look, the nascent dawn. Will it open a new day for you?"

Prostrate at his feet, Irène wept. A bitter dolor hollowed out her face and, in spite of the whitening dawn, she thought she was plunged in the most profound and terrifying night. Marcus leaned toward her; he caressed her black hair, which was spread over her shoulders, and consoled her gently.

"Anne sobbed," he told her, "because she had arrived. You will also arrive. Think about that unknown sister whose adventure I have told you. If you envy her fate you can appeal to me and you can put your hand in mine, as she did when I spoke to her on the edge of the wood, where I went to find her after someone had told me about her life, as I was told of yours. Reflect, Irène; do not exhaust your existence in futile expiation; no one ought to expiate, either for themselves or someone else. Remain in solitude today; you will find me again tomorrow."

He fell silent, placed his lips lightly on her forehead, and left her. She tried to stand up in order to accompany him to the threshold, but she had suddenly been invaded by such a terrible fatigue that could not do it, and watched him go through the doorway without retaining him by a gesture or a word.

"What have you done?" Claude said to Marcus, when they were some distance away. "You've killed her happiness."

"No, I've opened the door to it, and you'll soon see her with us. She is one of those that it is necessary not to allow to become bogged down in the mud of charity."

"Have you never been charitable?" asked Juste.

"The cordial in my flask and the bread in my bag have often helped someone, Juste, but I have given better than that thereafter. To weep over someone else's wounds indicates a sensible heart, to wash those wounds and bandage them testifies to a generous spirit, and one can do no less than dogs that lick one another's ulcers. Glorifying oneself for such a natural action, by making it the supreme, the noblest and finest action: that is what one cannot comprehend, if one knows the social necessity of charity.

"Charity is the Christian putrescence that maintains injustice. 'The poor will always be with you,' said the vagabond of Galilee, and his divinity has legitimated the evil. All the tyranny of the powerful reposes on that axiom; from it derives their passive cruelty, their inertia, their benevolence. To maintain the poor becomes the unique duty of the rich; to organize charity, to regulate alms: that is the entire social effort of the Christian world, and that effort recognizes the necessity of poverty; it perpetuates it by pretending to remedy it; in sum, it dispenses with justice.

"Oh, starvelings, paupers, how you have been duped! Your poverty has been glorified, it has been demonstrated to you that it is the finest of crowns, you have been told that you ought to be devoid of bread, like your god, and rejoice in it; the joy of Lazarus, who was content with crumbs, has been described for you, and you have believed all that, you have resigned yourselves to it; but you will only be free on the day when, taking down the images of the crucified liar, you spit in the face of your age-old suffering and tear up his slavish gospel."

"I understand," Claude murmured.

"And you, Juste, do you understand?"

"Certainly, Old Master. I am one of those you have aided and, better than a philanthropist would, I can understand the meaning of your words. But rather than continuing, permit me to speak to our friend. Claude, are we still far away from the bed you promised us?"

"This is the house," said Claude.

Juste uttered a sigh of satisfaction and went up the steps of the perron first, while the philosopher, before entering, gazed at the sun rising over Geronta.

XI

How Two Old Men Talked

IT had been a long time since Juste had slept in a bed. Accustomed to the straw of haystacks and barns, the grass of meadows, beds of dry leaves in the woods, or even the ground, he could not get used at first to the softness of the mattress, but he triumphed over that unease so victoriously that the following day's dawn found him still asleep. Marcus woke him up by coming into the room.

Juste opened his eyes, breathed in deeply, observed that his stomach was empty and his mouth dry, and said: "I'm thirsty."

"You're the most cynical of drinkers, Juste," the philosopher replied.

"I won't contradict that, Old Master, and if it's a vice to like drinking, I'm vicious. I wasn't born thus, though; I didn't cry for drink on opening my eyes, as Gargantua did, and in my youth the clink of bottles didn't make me fall down in ecstasy, like the son of Grandgoustier. Drunkenness has been the pleasure of my mature years, a rare pleasure, for I'm the most abstinent of drunkards and the most drunken of abstainers. Anyway, I have an excuse; I didn't take to drink, in accordance with the tradition, in order to forget. On the contrary, wine was, and still is, the benevolent stimulant of my memories and my dreams. I have a slack and lymphatic temperament and my brain has often borrowed from alcohol what my blood refused it."

While speaking, Juste had got up and got dressed. He ran to the window, saw that the sun was at the point where he had left it on going to bed, and showed an abundant sorrow.

"That star having been unable to stop in its tracks," he remarked, "I must conclude that I've slept since yesterday, at the least."

"Only since yesterday."

"That's sleeping too long, Marcus, and you see me sorry for it. I know nothing more stupid than sleep in happy periods. As much as I cherish it in hours of misery, I hate it in times of abundance, when it takes away the joy of living and sensing life."

"Do you like life that much, Juste?"

"Certainly! Is there anything more likeable? To open the mouth and the lungs freely in order to breathe the air is already a pleasure; it's a joy to see the daylight, a jubilation to move one's limbs. Do you know any greater satisfaction than that of acting, of exercising all one's functions—all of them, you understand, from the most base to the most elevated? Doesn't evil always come from hindrances, natural or artificial, put to that exercise; and isn't the supreme evil, in consequence, death, which brings the most powerful shackle, that one that can't be escaped? I have no appetite for death, and in reading the lives of philosophers I haven't found any as stupid as that Peisithanatos[1] who excited the

____

1 Peisithanatos [Death-Persuader] was the nickname attributed to the philosopher Hegesias of Cyrene, who lived in the third century B.C.; he is the subject of one of the stories in Lazare's first collection of stories *Le Miroir des légendes* (tr. as *The Mirror of Legends*).

Syracusans to go and having themselves from their fig-trees. But that's enough talk; is our host already awake?"

"I haven't seen him yet. Nevertheless, an abundantly laid table, glimpsed joust now in passing, seems to indicate that he got up before us."

"Why haven't you told me that already?" exclaimed Juste. "Show me the way, then, for it's unbefitting to make the dishes wait, inasmuch as, in spite of the proverb about sleepers, one thing is evident to me, which is that I haven't had anything to eat or drink for more than a day."

His companion's impatience made the philosopher smile. He refrained nevertheless from constraining him and took the starveling where he wanted to go. They found an aged valet in the dining room who placed himself at their orders and begged them on behalf of his master to take their places at table without delay.

Juste sat down, did honor to the wines and cold meats, and seemed to appreciate the choice. He sampled all the dishes, even returning to some of them, and when his hunger was appeased he uttered a sigh in which regret was mingled with satisfaction.

"There's no great appetite that isn't calmed," he said, "and I can't accustom myself to letting a pleasure fade away. I know that you'll reply to me that a perpetual pleasure would become a habit, and would then be impotent to procure us the desired sensation. It is, alas, that very infirmity of our nature about which I'm complaining! Our mucus membranes are truly insufficient; they tire and wear with a deplorable rapidity. Does the perfection of the senses have a place in your system?"

"Nothing in what you call my system opposes it; nevertheless, I abstain from the prophecies familiar to certain utopians. It would be easy to attribute to the regenerated human being the thousand senses of Micromegas; such predictions have the precious aspect of defying all verification; they therefore offer material for excellent speculations just as perfect as those on the nature of God.

"I once knew a Fourierist statistician whose ingenuity was satisfied in translating his master's hypotheses mathematically. He could say exactly what economic repercussions would ensue from the transformations of wine into a pleasant carbonated beverage. You're laughing, Juste? Is that any more stupid than announcing and describing scrupulously the beauties that will flourish on the day when the Paraclete arrives?

"That same statistician was very sad in thinking that he would not be able to eat each of the varieties of redcurrants produced by the planets Juno, Ceres and Pallas. And if anyone had brought him those fruits, the existence of which Fourier had discovered, he would not have been any happier, for he knew that if the Moon were not dead it would have engendered a fourth species, and that lost species would have procured him eternal regrets.

"You're still laughing, Juste? Do you find my statistician madder than you?"

"If that's where you're trying to get to, I grant you that your discourse is ingenious, and I admit myself vanquished. But I have no great merit in that; my optimism consoles me for everything, and I'm able to satisfy myself in thinking about future pleasures, since I have no lack of them!"

At that moment, they heard martial music resounding.

"What's that?" said Marcus.

"It's one of our regiments going to the drill-field," said the valet.

"An excellent opportunity to admire our army, Old Master, Let's go out on to the perron; we'll be ideally placed to watch them file past."

Juste immediately went downstairs to do as he said, and when Marcus came to join him he saw him sitting on the steps between two old men, to whom he was doing the honors of the place. One of them had a long and unkempt beard, the other was beardless and had a black eye-patch over his left eye. The philosopher listened to them.

"Handsome fellows!" said the old man with the beard.

"Heu, heu!" said the one-eyed man.

They looked at one another, and Juste interjected politely: "You don't know one another?"

"I'm a stranger," replied the bearded man.

"I only arrived here yesterday," said the one-eyed man.

"Permit me, then, to be the link between you," Juste proposed.

"Gladly," they said; and the bearded man said to the other: "You don't appear to admire those men?"

"We have better ones than that," exclaimed the old man with the eye-patch.

"How are your armies composed, therein?" Juste asked.

"We enlist the most robust of the peasants and the most vigorous of the workers, and our medical councils only give the uniform to men whose strength has been scrupulously tested."

"We do the same," said Juste. "Perhaps our physicians are more relaxed or less knowledgeable than yours. In any case, it hardly matters, for I imagine that you reserve for your soldiers the fate that we reserve for ours."

"What fate?"

"We routinely send them to fight savage peoples and conquer lands where they unfailingly perish of fever and consumption, when they aren't cruelly killed or atrociously mutilated. Their loss brings in compensation a few jars of rancid oil, elephants' teeth, a few quintals of rice, sugar or indigo, as well as the minimal sovereignty established over barbarian hordes and the satisfaction that consists of possessing more than one's neighbor. When that mode of elimination isn't sufficient, great wars are decided between traditional enemy nations, and, as the constant progress of civilization equips us with exceptional weapons, the elite of each people cannot escape an almost total massacre, to the profit of the generally debilitated plutocrats of the victorious nation."

"We do indeed act in the same way," said the one-eyed man, "but our objective is nobler than the one that you attribute to your fellow citizens, and we aspire uniquely to the grandeur and the glory of our fatherland."

"We don't give any other motive to our fashion of acting," Juste affirmed.

The bearded old man had listened silently to these remarks. "If I hadn't recently attended the sessions of your academies and scholarly societies, and read your newspapers and periodicals, I could believe that you were ignorant of the most elementary natural laws," he said, addressing Juste, "but I can suppose that your interlocutor's compatriots are unaware of them."

"We're not unaware of anything," declared the latter, in an arrogant tone. "Our scientists have penetrated the most secret arcana of nature."

"Then you don't know how to utilize their discoveries or take advantage of their doctrines. You must consider them as dilettantes and not as politicians. Your discourse shows me clearly that in your country, the coalition of the strongest, that necessity of social life, is poorly regulated, and that the conduct to adopt with regard to the weak, the useless and the harmful is not determined by just, practical and severe laws."

The one-eyed man smiled scornfully and made the observation to his opponent that he did not take any account of sentiments of pity, by which it would be inappropriate to be animated toward the debilitated, the suffering or the unfortunate.

"Evidently," he added, "we cannot prevent many of them from dying of hunger, cold or complete deprivation, in spite of seriously organized administrations concerned with equitable distributions, but there are few of our millionaires who do not, at the supreme moment, redeem the excess of their fortune by the foundation of hospices in which rickety or tubercular children are collected, along with lunatics and old men whose age renders them incapable of finding the morsel of bread necessary to delay their death."

"Monsieur," said the man with the long beard, "What you tell me testifies to an incredible naïvety. On the one hand, you claim to know what we call the natural order, and you affirm that you have enunciated in a satisfactory manner the law of the most apt, which ought to be the basis of government, but on the other hand, you show yourself to be indifferent to the elements from which you ought to draw your power, favorable only to the useful. It is natural that some of your Croesuses experience a pleasure in preciously conserving a few sorry, hunchbacked, deformed and knock-kneed individuals, and in comparing themselves to them . . ."

"Deplorable romanticism," Juste interrupted, "copied from the Emperor Commodus, who collected one-eyed lunatics, monopods, the legless, the obese, hunchbacks and those disfigured by hare-lips and unusual eczemas."

"The State," continued the speaker, untroubled by that interjection, "ought to abolish in your country those establishments where evil is cultivated, and grant those disgraced individuals the death that many of them await with anguish. Consider that your great sensibility might be satisfied by that, and it would be sagely extended. You would be conscious of sparing a large number of individuals from cruel suffering and painful cares, and they would be grateful to you for it, for only hereditary fears prevent them from killing themselves."

"And what would you do with morality?" exclaimed Juste.

"Yes," said the one-eyed man, supportively. "What would you do with that?"

"I would put it in accord with physical laws, whereas you place it outside them. In reality, we have no morality, but principles that we call moral because they permit us to live in conformity with the general order of things. Is the immortality of souls taught in your schools?" he asked, abruptly.

The one-eyed man burst out laughing, and Juste appeared to marvel at the question.

"You misunderstand me," said the bearded old man. "I'm not asking whether you believe in the immortality of the soul, but whether you are inculcated with the dogma. Your hilarity only proves that you are not. We carefully

refrain from such an error on our own account. We preach
to children the doctrine of the perpetuity of the individual;
nevertheless, we inculcate them with practical notions that
permit them, even if they are endowed with a feeble intelligence, to recognize that it is good to place oneself on
this globe, although transitory, in supportable conditions
of wellbeing .

"Selected tales, corroborated by examples, are sufficient
to attain that objective. Those young brains rapidly understand that a slice of bread and butter ought to be divided
into three rather than four, and that a robust comrade has,
in addition, the right to take possession of the totality
of the available rations. The despoiled are consoled, and
encouraged to accept that theft, by admirable descriptions
of celestial regions where they will be called to stroll subsequently. They are not left unaware, however, that if they
acquire more solid biceps, they too can aspire to terrestrial
wealth.

"As for the victors, they are enabled without difficulty
to understand the importance that there is for them in
restricting the number of possible consumers, and how the
disappearance of certain individuals is useful to the species. In spite of those lessons, in spite of the high esteem
testified to those who kill themselves voluntarily, generous
guests withdrawing discreetly from a feast that is inade-
quate, and in spite of the encouragement given to mothers
to abandon on doorsteps runts that are not collected, in
spite of all of that, mulish individuals are found, curious
to preserve and to see malformed children whose existence
is due to an inconceivable maternal tenderness or culpable
negligence kept alive. If we allow these people to persist,
as they have an excessive propensity for amorous pleasures,

they will populate our countries in a matter of years with an insupportable human vermin."

"You have doubtless not been embarrassed to bring a remedy to such a calamity," said the one-eyed old man, ironically.

"Monsieur has already given us too many proofs of the ingenuity of his compatriots for us to be able to doubt it now," observed Juste, politely.

"It is at this point," the imperturbable old man continued, "that we can usefully bring in the idea of glory and that of the fatherland. We compose our armies with those of whom we were speaking just now, the knock-kneed, twisted, hunchbacked, lame, sickly and idiotic, as well as those rendered decrepit by age, and when our assemblies of statisticians have established that the number of those infirm individuals is increasing in a disquieting fashion, an expedition is organized.

"Fortunately, in a distant country, there are dangerous shores, a mortal climate, and a population of cannibals who put to death a nephew of one of our kings a few centuries ago; periodically, we decide to take vengeance for that offense, which has never been repaired. A few appropriate speeches made in our public squares are then sufficient to excite an indescribable enthusiasm in our degenerates. They are conscious of being the designated avengers of national honor, and they depart voluntarily for regions from which they never return, in consequence of the difficulty of food supplies, the ferocity of our legendary enemies and the plagues endemic in the regions where they disembark. Thus we arrive by that means in suppressing the sad deformities and weaknesses of the human species."

On hearing the last words, the one-eyed old man could not master his indignation. He stood up, and seizing the other old man by the beard, he was about to abuse him with all his might; but Juste, whom that scene had rendered hilarious, seized him by the arm, mastered him, and calmed the fear of the unfortunate moralist, who, still tremulous, spoke sharply to Marcus, silent until then, asking him whether he did not approve of his ethics and did not find them in conformity with the modern givens of science.

The philosopher was getting ready to respond when Claude appeared. He saw the two old men; without saying a word, he grabbed a stick and threw himself upon them, belaboring them with blows, while they fled with an unexpected agility.

XII

The Garden of Speech

SURPRISED by that sudden attack, Marcus and Juste watched the two old men running away, and when they had seen them disappear around the street corner, they demanded an explanation from Claude of his strange conduct.

"Those two men," he replied, "are the most arrant rogues in Geronta."

"They're not foreigners, then?" exclaimed Juste, vexed at having been duped.

"Them! They're two former professors of philosophy fallen into disrepute, who employ themselves in the basest work. They belong to the police, but they're so well-known here to everyone, they've been seen so often drunk in the gutter or slumped against boundary-markers, that it's impossible to entrust them with any mission. Another role is reserved for them. They're charged with sounding out strangers who come into the city, provoking confidences from them, discovering their opinions and, if necessary, exciting their boldness by the liberty of their speech and the affected independence of their judgment. As they're adroit rascals, malicious and unscrupulous sophists, they excel in playing their roles. They wander through the streets and the squares constantly, and no inhabitant is unknown to them; fertile in ruses, they have a thousand ways of capturing the confidence of those who don't know them and making them fall into their traps." Addressing Marcus he added: "I arrived just in time; you were about to talk."

"And what would have happened?" said the philosopher.

"Perhaps you would have said the same to them as to the regulars of the Tavern of Hermes, and the two scoundrels would have denounced you without hesitation as guilty of having troubled order and attempted to pervert the public mind."

"How am I still at liberty in such a country?" said Marcus.

"You might make the acquaintance before long of the prisons of Geronta, if you persist in telling your parables in public," Juste concluded.

"It will be necessary, then, to pick up the traveler's staff and pitch our vagabond tent further away. It wouldn't be the first city from which I'd been expelled. Do you know a remedy for that, Claude?"

"If I didn't know one, I wouldn't have invited you to stay here. It would have been a fine offer on my part to welcome you only to constrain you to inaction and silence."

"Explain your means to us, then; Juste is waiting impatiently, for he finds himself comfortable in your house; your table and your wine please him, and he'd be sorry not to be able to testify his esteem for longer."

"Here it is," said Claude. "While traversing the island where I encountered you the other day, you admired the vast park enclosed by railings that occupies the part opposite the Palace. That park is known as the Garden of Speech. It was planted centuries ago, in the time when the country had kings, by a whimsical monarch who wanted to reserve in his kingdom, which he administered tyrannically, a refuge for liberty. That king was a dilettante, and in that quality, he inflicted the most grievous wounds on the monarchy. He had armies, a police and tribunals, thanks to which he suppressed any inclination to independence on the part of his subjects, but he found it ingenious and politic to permit the philosophers, moralists and economists of his capital to express their thoughts without constraint, and he had the Garden of Speech opened for them.

"He believed that he was establishing thus a kind of safety-valve, and rendering inoffensive ideas and theories that might become dangerous if they were compressed. Literate and subtle, that tyrant also experienced a great pleasure in listening to the debates of the literate, and the orators of the Garden of Speech had no listener more attentive than him. His calculation was disappointed; his own reign finished fortunately—which was perhaps the only goal he wanted to attain—but scarcely had he closed his eyes than the bourgeois and the rich, stimulated by the preaching of theorists of equality, roused the people, who overthrew the centuries-old throne and the feudal aristocracy that was its mainstay; then, having done that, they reduced their allies to slavery and elevated their power on the ruins of the past.

"Those positivist plutocrats, however, have maintained a relic of olden days. Regarding the Garden of Speech as the cradle of their fortune, they wanted to conserve it as it was. Nothing has changed, not the design of a single flowerbed, the arrangement of a clump of bushes, the ornamentation of a terrace, nor the placement of a hedge or a bowling-green. The statues of goddesses have remained as they were before, and the grottoes have been respected in the depths of which altars were raised to Cypris and the infant Cupid, as well as the ingenious fountains where the waters play.

"At the same time, the Garden of Speech has conserved its privileges. It is the only place that the police do not enter, the only one where people have the liberty to speak. There, Geronta's poets, fiction writers, esthetes, universitarians, and even revolutionaries come together; they recite their verses, read their novels and tales, expose their fantasies or their doctrines, and the sons of the richest merchants take pleasure in making the women who surround them shiver with the most subversive rhetoric. Their fathers are, in any case, in the audience and rejoice in the ingenuousness of their heirs, whose youth passes thus. No one thinks of attributing any importance whatsoever to the speeches of those fine intellects, but people are satisfied by their whimsy, their facile irony and their apparent profundity.

"Alongside them are also found the serious writers, the honor of the city, whom the brainless youths amuse themselves by jeering; the writers tolerate those idlers of no great range indulgently; they know that in the depths of those minds slightly stirred by youth, all respect and all prejudices are lurking, and beneath their satirists they divine their future disciples and future supports. They too have sown their wild oats, albeit in a different fashion, but with as much virulence, and they conserve in their midst a few decrepit octogenarians, terrible doctrinarians whom their adolescence attacked and their maturity venerates.

"However, among that crowd there are minds susceptible of opening to the truth; there are a few rare individuals whose hearts are noble and their souls troubled. Those, my friend, might be able to understand you. You can tell your parables freely, people will listen to them, and, if you let it be known that you have come from the north, you might even be applauded.

"You haven't mentioned that to me, Juste," said the philosopher, reproachfully.

"In truth, Old Master, I didn't think of it, and my excuse is that I've never frequented that place. I have a somewhat rustic appearance, and high society once frightened me. Today, travel has formed me; I've lost my juvenile timidity and learned enough to answer back congruently. I intend to show that soon, when we can remove the clamp on our tongue."

"Its weight scarcely inhibits you," said Claude

"I talk anyway," declared Juste gravely, "but I can say more and you, who are mocking, might obtain profit from my words. In the meantime, I don't know what we're doing on this perron. Marcus could have held forth here and rendered this new portico illustrious, but those of men would soon have come back." So saying, he went down the steps, followed by the philosopher and Claude, while adding. "I didn't think that the bearded man was stupid."

"You're not mistaken," said Marcus, "and in spite of the base profession he exercises, I believe that his sarcasm was sincere."

"Claude!" exclaimed Juste, slapping his thing. "Respond! Perhaps you've given a beating to the only independent philosopher in Geronta. The Old Master has opened my eyes, and I understand how cruel that cynic's satire was. What is his name?"

"Corax," said Claude.[1]

"It's necessary, then, that I find Corax again and that we empty a bottle together, for which the one-eyed man will pay, for the one-eyed man is inferior and it isn't him who could give a response of the subtle Corax. Corax, you duped me, and how I admire you for it! You've chosen an abject profession in order to be able to think freely, and you have the courage to play your role to the end, as young Lorenzaccio did.[2] What seeds you have deposited in the bosom of those you have expelled from this country! Perhaps there are some in whom the seeds will sprout, and if they ever encounter Marcus, the crop will be reaped. Corax, statues will be erected to you one day as to the martyrs of liberty; on the anniversary of your death people will come to place wreaths on your pedestal and honor you for being infamous. Claude, I suffer from the blows you gave Corax, and of having been the innocent cause of them. I shall be able to redeem my involuntary sin; I shall write the life of Corax, as the good Colerus wrote that of Spinoza."

Neither Claude not Marcus attempted to stop Juste, and Juste did not shut up. He was an amusing madman, an inexhaustible chatterbox, and perhaps he was only talking in order to excuse his perpetual thirst. He had a marvelous mastery of the art of transitions, and passed from one subject to another with surprising facility.

---

1 Corax [Crow, in Greek] was the name or nickname attributed to one of the founders of rhetoric in the fifth century B.C.

2 In Alfred de Musset's play *Lorenzaccio* (1834), whose hero is thus nicknamed as an insult but who goes on to assassinate a Florentine tyrant; the story is usually construed as a cynical commentary on the essential hypocrisy of the "July Revolution" of 1830.

"What difference is there, in any case, between him and the glass-polisher? The latter, to distract himself from his continual labor, throws living flies into spiders' webs; Corax causes men to fall into the judges' nets. If Corax had only written the *Ethics*, perhaps he wouldn't break his neck one night for having drunk too much—for Claude claims that he 's fond of drinking. Here, one can't put him in parallel with the gentle Benedict, who sustained himself every day with milky soup and a tankard of beer, but it's necessary not to criticize him either. He doubtless has the rule of consenting to do with the vulgar everything that isn't an obstacle to his goal.

"That's also one of my principles, and I acquired them in commerce with the little Jew of Amsterdam, who donated wisdom without accepting remuneration, and enriched himself more efficaciously than his coreligionists did. Corax is certainly one of his disciples. Why didn't I think of it sooner? Forgive me, Corax! You know that we have great advantages to obtain from the frequentation of men, if we proportion ourselves to them, as much as possible, and it's thus that we prepare benevolent ears for the truth.

"What power might you not have, Old Master, if you were a drunkard like me and Corax! You would see proselytes flocking to your sides in crowds, but you put yourself too far away from the poor and human passions. Oh, if you could convince Corax, what an apostle you would leave behind when you leave Geronta!"

At that moment the three pedestrians were traversing a small square cluttered by an active crowd pressing around merchants of comestibles who were holding their market there. In the fever of his improvisation, Juste, spreading his arms, collided violently with someone. He turned round, confused, and saw that his elbow had landed in the right eye of a short, fat quadragenarian woman whose left eye was already swollen and bruised.

The unfortunate individual began to utter piercing cries, by which Juste's compassionate soul was immediately saddened. He lavished the most delicate consolations on his victim, and, as she seemed sincere, he set out to prove to her that he had been an unconscious agent of Mother Nature in reestablishing on her visage the equilibrium and harmony troubled by the condition of her left eye.

"It's lucky I don't have a broken arm," muttered the lady. "You'd doubtless have thought it a duty to break the other, although I wouldn't have seen the utility of it."

That remark did not disconcert Juste, and he began to argue abundantly about the difference that separates the beautiful from the useful, and the possibility of combining those two elements of perfection. Claude could not help laughing and Marcus took pleasure in his companion's loquacity. How Juste did it, it was difficult for his friends to understand, stunned as they were by the flood of his words, but he soothed the woman to whom he was taking.

"I wish to Heaven" she said, "that the man who blackened my left eye had no more malice than you, and a heart as sensible."

Immediately, as much to repair his fault as out of curiosity, Juste hastened to ask the unlucky person how her left eye had been led to take on the colors of the rainbow, but as he asked that question he stepped backwards abruptly, shoved by a young man who went past at a run; he tripped, and ended up face down in a basket of eggs. The peasant-woman to whom the eggs belonged uttered savage clamors; her neighbors came running, and Juste, threatened by those harpies, only owed his salvation to the rapidity of his flight, the extreme velocity of his legs and the intervention of the philosopher, who took it upon himself to pay the expenses of the war.

While his friends were repairing his faults, Juste ran to the nearest drinking-fountain, where Marcus and Claude found him very busy washing his soiled face.

"Heaven be praised!" he cried to them. "The eggs were fresh; I could have fallen much worse. Tell me, Old Master, whether I don't have reason to be content with my lot, at least provisionally? Perhaps there's only that one honest farmer's wife in the square, and it's into the middle of her baskets that I fell. Who wouldn't believe in final causes? A worthy farmer's wife who abstains from selling bad eggs! It was necessary that she be recompensed. Now, hazard determines that I injure a passer-by, that a scatterbrain jostles me, that I fall over, and behold: the merchant sells her eggs to Marcus much dearer than she'd have sold them to the harpies of Geronta. Everything is connected, said the metaphysician who taught us morality at school, and everything collaborates to realize the obscure intentions of Providence. One thing about the adventure saddens me, though, and I permit myself respectfully to regret the impenetrable decisions of the divinity."

"What's that?" asked Claude.

"I'll never know why the quadragenarian woman had a swollen left eye."

While chatting thus they had resumed walking. Again, as they had two days before, they traversed the street of debauchery, whose taverns were closed at that matinal hour, and found themselves in the quarter of poverty again. In the sunlight, the tottering buildings appeared more abject, the leprosy of their walls stood out, extending from top to bottom, and the army of mildews emerging from the cracks invaded everything. Silence still enveloped the back-streets, but it was not the living silence of the night, the silence populated by the breath and sighs of the crowd. At dawn, doubtless, the houses had emptied, everyone departing to conquer the indispensable pittance, the bread that gives the strength to go back to the lodgings in the evening, in order to sleep and prepare to resume tomorrow the labor of yesterday.

There was no longer anything animated there but the muddy gutters slowly ferrying their filth, and a few meager stray dogs and cats lying on doorsteps rendered that solitude more lamentable and more poignant. The heat awoke ferments, excited putrescence and caused a sickening and insipid odor to emerge from the greasy soil, fetid mosses and viscous walls, through which, from time to time, an aromatic wave passed, the strong scent coming from the Oriental docks, before which the three companions, emerging from the filthy intersections, abruptly found themselves.

Facing them, the two giant arches of the entrance opened, and they saw in the depths the white quays where heavy trucks were arriving and departing and the blue and tranquil waters of the basins, which bathed the ships that were being loaded and unloaded. A din resounded compounded from a thousand noises: the squeal of pulleys, the tumult of clinking iron, the grinding of cranes powered by steam, the whistling of machines, the appeals of sirens, the whinnying and neighing of horses, and the formidable racket of the host of men populating the immense galleries that plunged endlessly into the black, scintillating shadow at intervals, beneath the pit of the water.

Marcus remained motionless for some time, filling his eyes and ears with the spectacle and the rumor of that powerful life. The vehicles departing incessantly were carrying cotton, silk and wool, greasy coal, sand, metals and wood to the factories whose dark smoke could be seen in the distance, and those incessantly coming back were bringing cloth and canvas, precious and vulgar glassware, furniture and ingenious machines: products transformed by human genius.

Instinctively, the philosopher's gaze moved above the enormous beams, above the roofs, and he saw beyond the river, which the massive buildings hid, the proud hills, with their villas, their theaters, their parks, their obelisks and their marble statues. They seemed to emerge from the docks, and really did emerge therefrom; it was there that their foundations were sunk, and if the heavy pillars and massive columns that sustained the edifice had been shaken, the city would have crumbled, and the frontons of its palaces would have been smashed on the granite jetty.

The shrill sound of a bell extracted him from his meditation; he suddenly heard a piercing clamor and men surged forth on all sides, running and howling. Ragged, pale and thin, seeking to catch up with those preceding them, the strongest repelled the weakest; they raced, mouths twisted and fists clenched and were engulfed in a narrow corridor, at the extremity of which, behind a grille, the bell-ringer was standing.

"Twenty!" he shouted. He opened a narrow batten and made the elect enter, one by one; then the watchmen set about chasing away the latecomers, who did not resist, and went away slowly, bleak and resigned.

"That's the appeal for supplementary workers," a tall, thin individual to whom he had not yet paid any attention said to Marcus. "You seem to have been watching that scene with interest, Monsieur, and I can understand that. I've been coming here every day for twenty years, and I never weary of admiring that scene; I even have the custom of bringing my pupils to this place frequently, and thus awakening their economic sense."

"You are . . . ?"

"A professor of political economics," said the unknown man, without letting Marcus finish.

"A curious science," said the philosopher.

"It's not *a* science, Monsieur, it's *the* Science! In fact, it's a metaphysics, for it penetrates the substance of things in order to establish their value; a mathematics, for it compares those values; a mechanics, since it measures desires, those forces, and gauges their intensity in accordance with the exchanges that satisfy them; a politics, since it brings men the fundamental law that regulates the harmony of societies, the law of supply and demand; and finally, it is simultaneously a principle of election and a morality, for it praises individual competition and initiative."

"Ah!" exclaimed Juste. "Why didn't my schoolmaster teach me political economics? He would have spared me ten years of college, and I'd be no less educated. However, he often brought us to walk past these gates, but the sight of those famished runners didn't provoke any excessive jubilation in him, and he didn't draw any lesson therefrom."

"What a poor brain your teacher must have had! From that spectacle I bring out my entire theory of the appropriation of wealth. That appropriation operates, in my view, in a single mode: liberty. You saw those men; no rule links then, no contract enchains them. They live on the special territory that might be considered by us as a microcosm; before them is the mass of wealth of which they might have a share; how can they attain it? One might imagine a superior power intervening at every hour and distributing a sort of ration to each of them, but what would become of human dignity? Where, henceforth, would be the principle of activity, of energy, and, in consequence, of intelligence? What would become of a people to whom it would be given to eat at fixed hours?"

"I don't know," said Juste, who thought he was being interrogated. "I've never known such a people."

"Is it not better," the professor went on, imperturbably, "to engage everyone only to count on his own strength and will-power, and only to see the doors open to the most agile . . . ?"

"And what becomes of the impotent?" Marcus interjected.

The economist looked at him, without seeking to dissimulate his scorn.

"Monsieur," he declared, "you will never understand political economics. Your question proves to me that you're a utopian, not a man of science. I have the honor of exposing to you a rational theory of the appropriation of wealth, and, without waiting for me to demonstrate the necessity of it, you ask me a question that can only satisfy your sensibility. I am not unaware of the woes of the weak, the poor and even those of the working classes, so worthy of interest; however, while not approving absolutely of Malthus, who has written that those woes have no remedy, I still have scruples about indicating the slightest reform. I firmly believe that the laws that preside over the division of wealth are a good as they are ineluctable. But in spite of forty years consecrated to the study of political economics, I cannot yet say whether the sack that contains flour is a fixed capital or a circulating capital, and you want . . ."

Indignation prevented the professor from finishing; he jammed his hat firmly on his cranium and, turning his back on the philosopher, he fled, raising his arms to the heavens.

"Old Master," said Juste, "it would have been better for you to blind a fat lady and break a few dozen eggs. Believe me, let's not linger here, and let's reach as soon as possible the beneficent garden where you can speak without exciting the fury of usurers, advocates and economists."

"Who can tell?" murmured Marcus, smiling; and, taking Claude's arm, he drew away.

XIII

The Speech in the Garden

WHEN the three men went through the gates, the garden was still deserted. Marcus was glad of that, for he was able to admire the décor at his leisure, and the décor was admirable. The park occupied the eastern part of the island, the one that ended in the prow of a ship and cleaved the waters of the river as if to go and disappear into the nearby sea. It was planted with centenarian trees, whose foliage palpitated under the lash of the midday sun and cut by broad lawns of dense lush grass; here and there, flowerbeds of various styles opened, designed by the most skillful of gardeners, and arbors covered in wisteria, clematis and honeysuckle loomed up.

Water features were distributed, guarded by Virgilian willows, and streams quivered in their beds of multicolored stones, descending broad marble steps every ten meters, over which the water slid like a silken fabric over white shoulders. The paths were bordered by trees of the rarest species, all those that could live in the open air in this climate. As for the plants of tropical regions and hyperborean regions, they were sheltered by immense greenhouses, which were decorated in a fashion representing the countries from which the multiple species that flourished therein had been taken.

There were African greenhouses there with their villages, their banana forests and their reconstituted undergrowth. Here there was North Africa, with its palm trees and sands, there the dense central forests, enclosing lakes in the middle of which nympheas blossomed, in a heavy and terrible atmosphere. There were Asian greenhouses in which one could pass from silent steppes to the splendors of ancient Taprobane, where strollers could enjoy by turns the Tibetan solitudes, the deserts of Arabia, the rice-fields of China, and Hindu jungles. The same variety was found in the American greenhouses, but the most beautiful were the Oceanian greenhouses, perfumed by spices and aromatic places, and populated by a strange flora and fauna.

"It's here that our speakers gather in winter," said Claude. "When the dog days arrive, they take refuge in the land of reindeer and hold their assizes alongside the huts of Ostiaks, Eskimos and Tunguses. But in spring, and during the first days of autumn, they remain in the gardens, where shelters have been constructed for them."

Marcus admired those shelters; there were porticos of porphyry built in the antique style, surrounded by lentisk bushes and oleanders, elegant rotundas sustained by svelte columns, galleries ornamented with statues and frescoes, bright grottoes, and countless pavilions whose architecture testified to the imitative tastes of the artists of Geronta, for one saw the genius of the most varied civilizations triumphing there, from the Greek temple to the Indian wigwam.

"I'd like," Marcus said when he had visited everything, "to see some monument of the Gerontan genre."

"There is no Gerontan genre," Claude replied, "either in painting, sculpture or architecture. Why would there be one? The inhabitants of Geronta employ their activity in acquiring riches, and those riches permit them to enjoy not merely the inventions of one people but everything that all peoples have found. A good Gerontan does not think of creating; what would be the point? Have not thousands of generations toiled with a view—and this is the entire Gerontan philosophy—to providing satisfactions to the citizens of Geronta, which is to say, to the inhabitants of the high city.

"Those people have come to believe that they represent the end-point of human evolution. Dead races, lost nations and vanished civilizations have prepared for the advent of Gerontans, not to work for themselves. Gerontans are made to savor, not to produce. Their forefathers have brought luxury and the means of material satisfaction to the highest degree of perfection, so they know that any effort to do better would only bring them fatigue, and they abstain.

"As for the refined individuals of Geronta, they refer to what the discoveries of antique decadences—Rome, Antioch, Alexandria—have imagined for them of sensualities, and resuscitate them. One becomes illustrious in renewing the marriage of Nero with Pythagoras, another, like Heliogabalus, in living with a courtesan and respecting her like a virgin, for they are impotent to invent even in debauchery. But what am I saying? You'll see and hear them all shortly."

While they were wandering thus over the lawns and pathways, the garden had become animated. The bowling greens were occupied by players, couples were wandering along the hornbeam hedges, groups were sitting under the arbors, and others occupying the porticoes and galleries. As the philosopher was tired, the three companions headed toward one of the park's large pavilions, built on a little promontory overhanging a pool of dormant water, the surface of which mosses had been allowed to invade. It had the form of an octagonal pagoda, all of whose faces were open, and access to it was gained via a spiral stairway.

"That's the pavilion of Eros, Claude had said when pointing it out, "the rendezvous of the poets, moralists and philosophers of amour. The caprice of a courtesan sheltered that college under a Chinese porcelain roof, where the ephebes, Bradamantes and false Agneses of Geronta unite every day."

When they went in, a numerous assembly was already crowding around a few men, who appeared to be the hosts of the place. The majority were old men; all the art of the perfumer could not hide that, even from the prejudiced eyes of their faithful adherents, and the cruel despair that they experienced was legible in their eyes; young disciples, whose minds they cherished but whom they envied, surrounded them and strove to imitate the laxity of their gestures, the preciosity of their attitude and the affected research of their mannerisms.

One of those masters was speaking, so the newcomers did not attract any attention. They sat down to one side. Juste listened briefly; then he shrugged his shoulders and relaxed into the soft armchair that he occupied. He went to sleep shamelessly.

Marcus listened to the conversation that had already commenced.

"Master," said a woman, "it displeases me to see you employing the word *deceive*. None of us can deceive her husband."

The man who was interrupted thus, a sexagenarian with excessively red lips and excessively dark eyes, an excessively insipid blond moustache, a clean-shaven chin speckled with spots and slightly flaccid cheeks, smiled complaisantly.

"The novelist Flavien," Claude whispered in the philosopher's ear.

"What do you mean by that, charming lady?" asked the novelist. "I surely ought not to conclude that you have no lover?"

A murmur of indignation was heard, and the faces of all the listeners expressed how insulting such a supposition would be.

"Let me interpret your words," Flavien continued. "I know, like you, that in our decrepit society, a wife is no more obligated to her husband than the husband is to the wife. A young woman is sold to an already mature man, or, which comes to the same thing, an already mature man sells his social advantages to the family of a virgin: that is marriage. More often than not, the engagement is reduced, on the part of the wife, to the promise of bringing a dowry, and on the part of the husband, to the assurance that he will be able to make that dowry fructify, and giving his wife the revenue in money and in social consideration. So, the wife only deceives the husband when she does not pay, and the husband only deceives his wife when he does not provide her with the agreed income."

An approving rumor ran around; people waxed ecstatic over the master's irony, his satiric and so truthful impertinence, and his questioner asked: "You don't admit exceptions?"

"I admit a thousand of them. Sometimes, in fact, the wife accepts the obligation to be faithful to her husband, but that is when she believes in marriage, in an order of sentimental things that only exists in amorous liaisons. If she then takes a lover, she is not deceiving her husband, her husband already having deceived her in not destroying that false conception prior to the marriage. In our society, so perfectly delicate and yet so oppressive for feminine individualities, marriage—this is the arcanum that you must penetrate, dear initiates—has no other goal than giving the wife more liberty for amour."

"And what can that liberty bring her," said one of the female listeners, clad in a loose mauve silk dress, languidly extended on a sort of chaise longue, "except for an illicit passion? The sole means that we possess to affirm to ourselves that we are not an item of merchandise, an object of exchange and traffic, the only fashion we can have of being conscious of our individual rights, the only manner in which it is possible for us to liberate ourselves from the chains with which Pharisaic morality charges us, is to make someone else the voluntary gift of our person."

"Yes," Flavien approved, "Amour, the father of liberty, satisfied desire victorious over slavery; the liberty of amour and liberty by amour, that was the guiding principle of many heresiarchs. According to many men, the liberation of the flesh has been the emblem of the liberation of the spirit, and even its prologue. When the flesh is enslaved, the spirit is debased; all license for the flesh is also license for the spirit. That was the thought of the Adamites, of Mark, and the excessively calumniated Carpocrates,[1] and

----

1 The Adamites were an early North African Christian sect best-known for nudity during their religious celebrations; Carpocrates was

I have read in a very old chronicle a story that shows how vivacious and persistent that doctrine remains, and on what excellent examples we can support ourselves in order to return it to honor. I shall tell it one day."

"No!" cried impatient voices. "Now, right away!" And supplicant hands were extended toward the novelists.

"You want that?" he said, in a dying and slightly broken voice. "So be it; listen to me." He smoothed his blond moustache with a long and excessively supple white hand, and he narrated, in a rhythmic, singsong tone.

---

the founder of a Gnostic sect in Alexandria charged with libertinism by its detractors, as was standard practice in diatribes. The evangelist Mark was said by legend to have founded the Alexandrian Church.

XIV

The Free Spirits

ETIENNETTE DE CORTENBERG, who married the Seigneur de Fourquemont, was the most beautiful young woman in Hainaut, so beautiful that her beauty served to make her fortune, a very fortunate thing for her, for her father was scarcely able even to give her the adornments of a young wife. She had consented without repugnance to be the wife of the Seigneur de Fourquemont, who was rich and was madly smitten with her.

The Sire, although already nearing fifty, was still seductive in appearance, in spite of the fact that he had made war here and there and had adventures; he had an almost juvenile briskness and his face, although rude, was not lacking in attractions. Etiennette judged him to be a good and loyal knight, and as she had been told that her future husband had a few of the brutal traits of bravery and heroic folly that captivate simple women, she regarded him with sympathy and made no difficulty about giving him her virginal affections. She was, in any case, flattered to have conquered by means of her beauty such a wild companion, rebellious until then to amour, who seemed only to have delayed his fall in order to be better enchained.

Although she felt a legitimate pride in her conquest, she was not passionately amorous of a man who, after all, for an eighteen-year-old, was only an old man. In a word, her vanity was captured far more than her heart and her senses, and if she could not contain her joy, it was at the thought of quitting the sad house of her father to become the chatelaine of Fourquemont.

That joy was of short duration. The Seigneur de Fourquemont, although he was an amorous knight, was not a courteous and facile lover. He was uncivilized and he was unable to organize his passions. As soon as he had possessed his wife, as soon as he had lived with her for a few days and thus understood the price of the treasure he had acquired, his tenderness gave way to the most redoubtable, the most ferocious and the most vigilant jealousy. He became the rigid accountant of Etiennette's smiles and gazes, he demanded an account of all her words and all her deeds, and reproached her constantly for not devoting them all to him. He aspired to pass from the rank of spouse to that of idol, and wanted to be served by his wife like a god by a priestess, or a priest by a slave.

Etiennette became her husband's serf, the vilest of serfs, since she was obliged to submit to him not only her body but also her spirit and her will. Under the harsh regime of suspicion and the yoke of jealousy, her affection for the man that she had admired as a heroic knight whose renown had flattered her pride, evaporated like the perfume from a broken bottle, and her soul was charged with anger and hatred.

As she was not sensual, she did not think of deceiving her husband. What was most odious in her life, in any case, was not being unjustly suspected but not being free, and being treated like a captive. An unexpected circumstance came to modify her ideas, and caused her to conceive life differently.

After three years of that existence of a reclusive jailer, the Sire de Fourquemont, obliged to go to Brussels, took his wife, whom he did not want to leave alone in the manor, with him in a perfumed month of April. In Brussels, Etiennette was less enchained, her husband not wanting to be regarded by everyone as a jealous man—for, by virtue of a singular phenomenon, his vanity would have been humiliated if he were obliged to make the admission, implicitly, that he was not sure of his wife. Etiennette, therefore, had the appearance of liberty. She was able to go out every day, accompanied by a few followers, in order to attend to her devotions.

One morning, as she was returning to her lodgings, she heard clamors resounding; the deserted streets suddenly filled up with a tumultuous and noisy crowd, a hetero-geneous crowd of knights and artisans, clerics and lay-men, who were running and shouting, clamoring a name: "Bloemardine! Bloemardine!"[1]

The flood carried Etiennette and her followers away. Her curiosity, in any case, kept her from resisting. Thus pushed, half-consenting, they arrived in front of the town hall. There, a woman was sitting in a silver armchair raised on a small platform. At the sight of her, the memory re-

---

1 Bloemardine was the nickname of Heilwige Bloemart (c1270-c1335), a quasi-gnostic mystic who belonged to a powerful Brussels family, whose protection seems to have shielded her from the Inquisition. In Jacques Collin de Plancy's oft-reprinted *Dictionnaire infernal*, where Lazare probably found her, she is represented as an enthusiastic supporter of free love, but that description of her ideas is based on dubious sources.

turned to Etiennette of a prophetess popular throughout Hainaut, whose doctrine no one had been able to explain to her. She understood that the woman sitting on the seat of pure silver was Bloemardine, and she felt joyful without being able to understand why.

She gazed at the woman that the common people called blessed. She was tall and slim, her face inflamed by ardor. She was not beautiful; she had a willful chin, thick and voluptuous lips, and a broad, slightly bulbous forehead. The lower part of the face was that of a courtesan, the forehead and eyes those of a saint. She was surrounded by young men and young women; someone near Etiennette said that they were the Free Spirits; that was what Bloemardine called the faithful of her church.

When the noise had calmed down somewhat, those adolescents shouted at Bloemardine: "Speak!"

Bloemardine rose to her feet, made a gesture, and, silence having fallen abruptly, she spoke.

She began by glorifying carnal amour, created by God and given to humans as a joy and a kind of wellbeing ; she praised the pleasures of the flesh, saying that they were beautiful and noble and that it was criminal to put shackles on them. Then she spoke about the tenderness of souls, of seraphic and pure love; she showed that the spiritual ardor in question was the daughter of carnal passion and that the latter sustained it, as the flesh sustains the spirit. In its turn, seraphic love was the parent of the spirit of liberty, the breath and flame of the world, the inspiration of the will: the spirit of liberty that would reign as master over the earth on the day when all constraint would be abolished, and all law save for the law of amour destroyed. She concluded by saying that the free gift of her body was for a woman the symbol of the liberty that she ought to enjoy, and, so to speak, the preface of her liberation.

Etiennette did not hear any more; those words had struck her as lightning striking: a sudden light had appeared to her. She fled, pursued by the voice of Bloemardine, returned to her dwelling meditating on the words of the inspired woman and, her desire illuminating her, she recognized that the only fashion of doing the work of a free woman was to be unfaithful to her husband.

She found in that means a double advantage: she avenged herself and affirmed her right not to be enslaved. She wanted to be liberated by passion, and a woman who thinks thus does not remain for long with a fallow heart; thus it was for Etiennette—and following the advice of Bloemardine, she was able to give license to her flesh to liberate her captive will.

Thus Flavien concluded. The women were delirious; they turned their ecstatic faces, their eyes revulsed, toward the aged erotic rhapsodist, who dominated the troop of his handmaidens complaisantly. They all extended to their beloved master their entire bodies, the homage of which he would not have been able to accept, and their mouths opened, while their flat chests strove to swell their corsages.

One among them, however, had remained upright, her lips disdainful and contracted, her forehead striped by a harsh and haughty crease. Flavien looked at her, perhaps taking pleasure in admiring that tormented face, and suddenly, he asked her: "What's the matter with you, Flavie?"

"The horror of the base things you say," she replied. "Oh, these creatures, they still believe in the old folly that your ignominy propagates. What a wretched doctrine: to abdicate in order to liberate oneself! Whether it enslaves her to the will of a husband or curbs her under the passion of a lover, amour cannot liberate a woman. It is merely to choose our master, to weave ourselves the garlands that bind us. Sensuality enchains us, as procreation enslaves us. Only one woman is free: that is the virgin, and virginity is the unique condition of our liberty. Neither lover not mother: virgin! To keep far away from oneself the pack of tyrannical desires, not to soil one's purity, to remain lily-white, devoid of any stain, to flee filthy caresses . . ."

A voice interrupted her; someone had stood up facing her and said: "Nothing is impure for pure hearts."

"Why," exclaimed Juste, who had just woken up, "it's our friend the mystagogue! He's going to tell us another story of doves. Do you know that fellow, Claude?"

"Certainly. It's Aure, the beloved poet, the one whom Gerontian ephebes follow recklessly. Admire him, Marcus, he's the leader of a school. He's the father of those who pick up their lyre to sing the sweetness of the Eucharist or the frightening mystery of the Trinity; he has engendered the latest poems, those that are rutilant with the gold of monstrances and whose hemistiches exhale incense; lustral poems, hymns, psalms and litanies, punctuated by the re-sponses of the mass, celebrating and interpreting the holy sacrifice in incoherent and ejaculatory rhythms. Behind him march the enervated adolescents, the primitive hyster-ics, the delectable sadists, the mildly sacrilegious and the entire swarm of the delirious and the satanic, the mages who practice that literature of excommunicated sacristans, fluent and agitated beadles. It's the flower of the race, the last branch of the tree whose buds one dares not touch, so much does one sense them swollen by putrescence, so much does one fear that they might burst between the fingers, spreading their sticky and fetid flux. What will come after them if the people down there do not begin to march?" And he indicated, in the distance, the low city groaning in its labor.

"The people down there are asleep," said the philosopher.

"Will they not wake up?" Claude murmured.

"Patience; already they are agitating in their excessively narrow beds; obscure dreams are troubling their sleep. When the sun, which is scarcely born for them, strikes their eyelids, they will get up."

"Listen! Listen!" cried feminine voices. "Aure is going to speak." And the thinnest and palest of the equivocal creatures in loose dresses gasped with emotion in awaiting the speech.

Aure began.

XV

Pure Hearts

LET me praise before you Agapia the prophetess, disciple of Mark, master of Priscillian,[1] for Agapia came to declare to men that the body, abominable matter, can no more sin than a brute can sin, and that our soul alone is accountable for sins. Let us praise Agapia, who inspired amour and spirit; let us forget that the Church made her a heretic and love her because she knew how to love.

She lived in Spain, in the first centuries of ardent, naïve and often subtle faith, that epoch when the Christian lands still retained the perfume of compassionate bounty that the apostles and the first martyrs had spread there. Agapia's soul was embalmed in pity. She went into towns

---

1 Priscillian was a fourth-century Christian ascetic accused by his critics of Gnostic tendencies who was eventually charged with sorcery and forced to confess under torture to various licentious practices before being executed. The name Agapie [Agapia] is attributed by some writers to a Christian virgin of the third century, but the association of the name with Priscillian might derive from a misunderstanding of Saint Jerome's criticism of him, which criticized his alleged misunderstanding of the Christian *agape* [love-feast]. As before, the invocation of the Evangelist Mark in association with allegedly Gnostic ideas is probably significant.

preaching the tenderness that melts hearts, soothes spirits and permits them to communicate in the infinite ocean of love. She attached herself to the seduction of women, and women gave themselves to her easily. When she had conquered a troop of auxiliaries, she told them that henceforth, in order to symbolize the flame with which they burned for others, as well as the link that attached them to their initiatrix, they would be called the Agapetes, and she sent them to men.

As Agapia had instructed them, so the Agapetes instructed the young men; they taught them that it was necessary to forsake metaphysics and dry doctrines, for when they possessed pure love, they would have the key to the world.

All the adolescents were seduced by them, and young women were scornful of themselves for only knowing egotistical conjugal love; so, when the Agapetes had spread their propaganda, adulterous couples were seen wandering on the outskirts of towns, in gardens, on river banks, in meadows and in the woods, seeking the prelude to universal love in the joys of carnal passion.

But a terrible rumor soon went up against Agapia and her disciples: the wrath of deceived husbands, the dolor of betrayed lovers, the despair of neglected mothers, the indignation of matrons and old men, and the malediction of clerics who sniffed the odor of conjoined flesh palpitating above sanctuaries. Agapia was accused of corrupting youth by teaching it to love, and she was summoned before a Sanhedrin of priests and laymen to justify herself.

She came before the tribunal, escorted and surrounded by enlaced couples of Agapetes, whose voices united to glorify her, celebrating her wisdom and her virtue, for

Agapia was not subject to the weaknesses of her congregation; she was chaste and only ardent in spirit. She was interrogated regarding her doctrines, and in response she praised Love, the same, according to her, as the Word: Love, the principle and end of things, the reign of which was announced; the just Love that would come to judge humans and redeem them.

When she was asked why she authorized license, she replied that she did not permit it or forbid it, that passionate love could, for some, be the vestibule to spiritual love, and that it was, in any case, the master of young and simple souls. She was reproached with being prey to the demon of impurity. She stood up then, and, criticizing those who claimed to be her judges, she said: "Nothing is impure for the simple, the gentle and the good; nothing is impure for pure hearts, for only the spirit can fail, and whatever it does, the body is always innocent . . ."

"Let's flee," said Juste, fearfully. "I know that rhapsody. We only just have time to escape the incantation to pure hearts. If you want to know the end of the story, I'll tell you that, naturally, Agapia was condemned by the judges, whom our dear mystagogue is going to curse, probably in rhythmic prose."

When they were on the steps of the staircase, Claude said: "Still, he's one of the less terrible, and if he's a plague on the brains of those sick individuals we just heard clucking with pleasure, he doesn't lack a certain ingenuity. The others, the disciples, are worse. They're the lock-keepers of pity, the glorifiers of naïve stupidity and imbecility; they celebrate simplicity of mind, castigate the evil of understanding and scorn the science that desiccates and leaves their poor souls unsated. They praise the divine goose-girls whom heaven favors with its revelations and see in a cretin who has faith the ideal of humanity. They're worse than old Flavien, who has nurtured them. At least that ancestor limits himself to endless rambling about amour, erotico-sentimental arguments and passionate casuistry. How many volumes he and his peers have written, always turning in the same circle, never finding a solution, or even an idea."

"Is that not fatal?" Marcus observed. "And is it not inherent in the fashion in which civilized people have understood womanhood? For centuries, literature and art, poetry once, the novel now, have lived on the principle, the dogma, of the essential, original, fatal, incurable misunderstanding between man and woman. The most various reasons have been found for that misunderstanding, psychological, moral and physiological; people have sought remedies for it when they have not despaired. If a panacea had been discovered, half of lyric poetry would not exist.

"The poets have taken account, unconsciously, of the scourge that would fall upon them if that misunderstanding were one day to cease, and they have been the propagators of the evil. If the fate of the human species is not to be divided into two enemy camps, howling and lamenting mutually; if its destiny is, as I believe, to be united, then poets are the worst of men, the deadliest of animals. As that race seems to me to be ready to disappear, for the peoples are too old henceforth to sing the praises of their passions like primitives and savages, among whom song is a stimulant to action or a consolation. I conclude that our descendants will be fortunate, because they will have established reasonable relationships between them and their companions. In reforming society they will reform amour, and that reform will be operated pedagogically.

"On the one hand, men in ridding themselves of lyricism, will rid themselves of feminine fetishism; they will no longer consider their lovers as ferocious goddesses only susceptible of being satisfied by the offering of bloody flesh. On the other hand, women will lose the sense of their divinity and will no longer make the demands that the divinity in question entails. Only then will amour be conceived as the equal exchange of sentiments between two equal individuals.

"Today, perfect love, such as all individuals will practice it one day, only exists in the state of an exception. The relationships between lovers are the relationships of master and serf, or those of priest and god. Amour is no longer a passion, it is a cult, the last of religions, with its dogmas, its rites and its follies; it has its hierodules and its hierophants, its mystics, its heretics and its fanatics. Commonly, it is the woman who is the idol, it is at her feet that one prostrates oneself, but sometimes the man refuses the adoration, and there are then two ways to go, either to flee into solitude or to dominate his turn. Amour becomes a vengeance on both sides. The woman avenges herself with refinement, and even with cruelty, for the social, moral and intellectual inferiority in which the male maintains her, and the latter avenges himself brutally for having yielded to an inferior.

"In the Christian world, the woman is a slave god, debased by the religion, which, in contriving the apotheosis of the virgin, leads to the scorning of the mother and the abasement of amour. In other societies, she is scarcely considered anything but a producer of children or a beast of burden. So long as we live on those equally barbaric conceptions we will not know happiness and we will engender debilitated brains, the likes of Aure, Flavien and Flavie."

He had paused, in order to speak, beside the pool, whose silver reeds inclined gently. He contemplated the loveliness of the mosses, and under their delicacy he saw the decomposition of the waters, the putrescence that enabled them to live and was only manifest by dark patches making holes here and there in the mantle of green velvet that covered the stagnant pond. They had scented the exhalation up above, beneath the porcelain roof: a sickening odor that musks could not mask.

If I said that to them, he thought, *they would probably find one of those lunatics clairvoyant enough to extract a symbol from it.*

At that moment, he divined a presence behind him; he turned round and saw Irène.

"I was there," she said.

"Are you coming with me?" he asked.

"I don't know," she replied. "The heart of little Anne was stronger than my heart. Let me follow you and hear you. Perhaps I'll understand completely one day. It's necessary for me to walk in your shadow before confronting the light." As he extended his hand, she begged: "Don't retain me," while a frisson ran through her body.

He said nothing, smiling at the alarm of her fearful soul, and he watched her go away through a long avenue of oaks that were already darkened by the flight of the sun. Dusk was falling; the air, saturated with scents coming from the greenhouses, was becoming heavy; peacocks perched on the frontons of porticoes or wandering on the terraces of galleries, uttered desperate clamors; a kind of dust was falling from the foliage and charging the atmosphere. The rumor of the river was becoming audible, and that of the city, which was confused with it above the island.

"Shall we go see life?" Juste proposed. "The artifice of this society displeases me, and if you have no objection, Old Master, I'll vagabond tonight and debauch myself a little. I know a mariners' inn where one eats fried fish and drinks sharp wine. That will be a change from the Pavilion of Eros, where I had a good nap."

"Do as you wish, Juste. If Claude is agreeable, we'll walk together this evening, and we'll come back here tomorrow."

XVI

Old Thoughts and Prophetic Dreams

When Marcus and Claude left the house the following afternoon to return to the Garden of Speech, Juste, who had abandoned them the day before, had not yet reappeared. That disappearance did not surprise the philosopher. He knew that his companion was a scrupulous man, who, having promised to get drunk, must have kept his word. Doubtless he had now woken up in some tavern and they would find him again when they returned to the lodgings in the evening. They set forth, therefore, without anxiety, and made the right decision, for, when they arrived at the entrance to the bridge, they saw the night-owl in the distance, waiting for them, sitting on a stone bench. He stood up as his friends approached, came to meet them, and before anything else spoke to Marcus.

"Old Master, don't tell me that my face bears the traces of debauchery. Perhaps it is a little more lit up than usual, but that's the effect of nocturnal wine. Nocturnal wine is malicious, and I've noticed that it colors more than diurnal wine. Why? I don't know, and I need a few more years of study to find out. The one I drank last night was sharp, as I told you, and although its acidity is sometimes pleasant

"

to taste it is bad for the complexion, reddening faces, and I don't advise flighty women and yesterday's suitors to make use of it."

"Perhaps that's advice that you ought to be the first to follow," said Marcus.

"Have you a special horror for sharp wine? In order to be agreeable to you, then, I'll renounce it, all the more so as I've been disillusioned. I cherished it twenty years ago, though, and I was obliged to summon up all my memories last night in order to be able to drink it. Even so, I would have found it bad if Corax hadn't encouraged me, claiming that the sensation might awaken other correlatives."

"You've seen Corax?" asked Claude.

"Corax is my friend," Juste replied. "I looked for him, I found him, and, following my program, the one-eyed man, who was with him, paid our bill. Marcus, it's necessary for you to see Corax again; he is such as I imagined him, ingenuous and simple. The mariners in whose midst he has come to live as a comrade gave him their affection. They're not prejudiced, and the profession he follows appears less blameworthy to them because they can't experience any inconvenience from it. In any case, those worthy folk are guided by a superior principle against which, in these times of ferocious struggle, any other principle is broken."

"What's that?" asked Claude.

"One has to live. You, Old Master, who is virtue itself, must understand that."

"Certainly," replied the philosopher, "and I can't contradict them. The goal of human beings—the sole unique goal—is to live. It's merely a matter of understanding life. For your mariners, it doubtless consists of fulfilling the essential functions of the human machine, and they know no other ends than that. They're therefore right to aspire to it by all means, and it's their very persistence that will permit them to attain other notions—notions such that they'll be able, in order to realize a better ideal, to renounce sustaining their existence by methods susceptible of thwarting that ideal.

"They place the excellence of life in duration; a good life for them, is a long one. For others, excellence is in the quality, in the beauty of the work accomplished. The evil comes from the fact that those two conceptions can't yet be brought into accord; the good and justice will be realized one day by their harmony, and the search for that harmony is our endeavor. What would Corax say to that?"

"Corax would approve. However, he'd find your two categories too clear-cut. Corax is a man of nuances, and he scorns the one-eyed man because the one-eyed man doesn't see everything; he scorns him, however, as a symbol, and loves him as an individual. All of Corax's spirit is in subtle distinctions. It's by a thousand arguments that he establishes his equilibrium. He succeeds in justifying his profession by his philosophy, and his philosophy by his profession, and he redeems the evil that he does by means of the good to which he aspires."

While talking they had gone into the garden; they were now chatting in a flowery section ornamented by stone fountains and little bowling greens, in the middle of which stood graceful goddesses: Pomonas, Floras and amiable Ceres.

"To what endeavor does Corax devote himself when he finishes his labor?" Marcus asked.

"To an essential endeavor, without which yours would remain futile. He reveals to the mariners their poverty, makes them understand their distress and teaches them to hate. Corax wasn't born to preach love, but tell me whether love can ever be made without hatred. Hatred is necessary to tear down and love to rebuild. That's what Corax thinks; don't you cherish him now, Old Master?"

"You told the truth the other day, Juste; Corax is a saint. He has chosen obscure work, patient and ingrate labor, of which the memory escapes human minds. The heroes of the revolution that will come one day, the necessary avengers and destroyers, will have been engendered by Corax, but the name of Corax will be forgotten, for one only remembers the builders, those who carve the stones of future edifices. One morning, someone comes, and knocks down the worm-eaten house with a pickax, and his memory is glorious; he is, however, the heir of the Coraxes who have undermined the foundations, crumbled the cement, corroded the beams and shaken the walls. The new humanity might make him the symbol of the forgotten workers, but the name of Corax will have sunk into darkness. I know all that, Juste. But I won't see Corax, and it's not good that we see one another; the time hasn't come for us to meet." He interrupted himself suddenly: "But where are you taking us, Claude?"

"Do you know old Testis, Juste?" asked Claude, by way of response.[1]

"Who doesn't know him? Isn't he the only man in Geronta who has seen, it's said, the last hours of trouble and resistance in the city henceforth enslaved?"

---

1 As well as its more familiar reference, the Latin word *testis* [witness] is also the root of the verb to testify.

"Is it to him that you're taking me, Claude?" the philosopher exclaimed.

"Yes, but I don't think it's possible to interrogate him. Testis is dead to everything. His pupils are extinct and, of the thoughts of old, his mind has only been able to retain a mysterious story, a legend, dream or reality, which some take pleasure in making him relate. I want you to hear that troubling tale; it has stirred my adolescent soul, it has shown it a tragic past and a better future."

They had not quit the flower-garden and at the turning of a path Marcus saw a few men sitting next to a grotto garlanded with miniature roses. They were surrounding a frail old man with the delicate and desiccated head of a bird, a body still upright but whittled away, almost drawn out.

"That's Testis," said Claude. "In this garden, where he is brought every day, people come to see him with a curiosity mingled with envy and the fear caused by the unique debris of a vanished world. Those who contemplate him experience in his presence the fetishistic respect accorded to relics."

They drew nearer; Claude put his hand gently on the ancestor's shoulder.

"Talk to us, Testis," he begged.

Testis nodded his head; the shadow of a smile wandered over his withered lips, and in a strange, distant voice, a voice of dream, blank and as if muffled, he spoke slowly.

I remember that dawn. The sky, sown with stars, lit up in the east with a light that extended gradually; the river awoke, it broke its nocturnal silence, and the noisy waves were populated with indecisive phantoms of mist. Frost blanched the bare branches of the trees and covered the ground with a crystal carpet that crunched under the feet of the stroller and troubled the matinal calm.

I went as if in a dream; sometimes I stopped, I leaned over the parapet of the quay, watching pale, soft galleys coming toward me, floating on the water; I imagined them decked with silver brocade, strewn with satin cushions on which sleeping nymphs lay; but a damp breeze rose, the breath of which dispersed the fragile ships, and I no longer saw anything but the innumerable flocks of swans flexing their necks and wings in accord with the rhythm of the vanished vessels.

I thought I was the master of a dead city, and when I arrived at the bridge I stopped, surprised; a long, veiled, motionless form was leaning against a lamp-post, under the vacillating flame. I approached soundlessly, fearful of frightening the unexpected apparition and causing it to vanish like those, doubtless her sisters, borne by the fleeting galleys.

When I was before her, I saw her join her hands in supplication, and I heard her voice imploring pity. I reassured her; for me, she parted the muslins that enveloped her, and appeared to me, touching and beautiful. She was wearing a ball gown in mauve silk embroidered with pearls, a robe with a split neck-line that opened over a gracile and virginal cleavage, and fell over shoes that the ice had covered, a robe of times past, of the court.

Her coiffure was not in harmony with the slightly stilted formality of the costume; its expert artifice had come undone; some unknown shock had destroyed its architecture, and the blonde hair, scattering, spread over her shoulders, covering her figure, while crazy wisps snaked over her face, dominated by a few persistent torsades. The face of the unknown woman was child-like and thin; her cheeks were emaciated, and her profound, sparkling and moist eyes animated her expression, which a red and fleshy mouth rendered even more puerile.

I saw her thus, trembling and fearful, seductive in her emotion; I held out my hand to her and, reassured, she started to walk beside me, with the little leaps of a frightened bird. Sometimes, terror appeared to grip her again; she escaped from my grip and fled along the causeway; then, calmed, or perhaps frightened by the solitude, she came back.

Gradually, however, her hectic and fearful humor disappeared; her stride, rapid at first, slowed down; she leaned more heavily and more confidently on my arm, and soon, thinking that I had conquered her, I questioned her.

"Who are you?" I asked her. "What were you doing on the water's edge, forsaken and shivering, clad in that outdated robe, and from what ball have you emerged?"

She started laughing, a laughter that resonated with the sound of an antique harpsichord, and clapped her hands to express her joy.

"You think that I've been dancing," she said, "and that I'm wearing a hired costume. You don't know my story then, and you've never heard mention of me?"

I made no reply, and the child went on.

"Oh," she said, "mine is a strange story, and doubtless you won't believe it. It doesn't matter; I'll tell you anyway; if you're a gentleman, you'll at least pretend to lend credence to it."

As I affirmed that I would give faith to the least of her words, she drew me close to a lamp-post and, showing me her hand, she pointed out a long scar on the palm.

"You see that wound; all the eldest children of my family have conserved the mark since the adventure of our ancestor. You know her, that ancestor, the memory of whom is lost in legendary darkness. She lived in forgotten times, when the divine fays still roamed the plains and answered the appeals of mortals. One day, while she was threading wool on her distaff, the spindle pierced her skin and she slept for a hundred years, until the morning when the prince that her dreams had formed during that century came to wake her up. My name is Aurora, as her daughter was called,[1] and my brother, whose name was Day, died a long time ago. For I'm older than you," she added, shaking her head mischievously, and pretending that her voice was hoarse.

I sketched a compliment, but amazement prevented me from speaking, and I made the decision to remain silent.

"Much older than you," she went on. "I lived in the epoch when queens were shepherdesses,[2] when the crooks that starveling shepherds brandished on the hills were ornamented with ribbons; I knew the kings who forged iron without hearing the resonant hammers of grim black-smiths. Don't be astonished by my grave tone; if I have

---

1 The heroine of Charles Perrault's *La Belle au bois dormant* (tr. as "The Sleeping Beauty") is not named, but in the 1890 ballet with music by Tchaikovsky she is named Princess Aurora; the reference to this Aurora being the "daughter" of the original can thus be construed as ironic.

2 Marie Antoinette, notoriously, liked to dress up as a shepherdess to play in the Petit Trianon; this comment thus confirms the intended allegory of French history.

the appearance of a blonde and cheerful little girl, I have the soul of a disabused grandmother. Have I not seen the horrors of massacres, the wrath of the crowd in revolt, the abominations of firing squads? And my heart was so bruised that one evening, very dark and very lugubrious, I invoked the benevolent fay who had once lent her aid to the beautiful sleeper.

"She responded, and came to sit at my hearth in the garb of a pauperess, for she had been obliged to leave her chariot hitched to flamboyant dragons at the entrance to Geronta, and the sake of prudence, she had not been able to wear her gold and silver robe. I huddled against her breast and begged her to put me to sleep until the time when the sun would shine on happiness returned, when men would be mild and fraternal with one another.

"'You're asking too much of me,' she replied, 'and if I granted your wish, my dear Aurora, you would risk sleeping eternally; but what I once granted your ancestor I can also grant you.' She kissed me softly over the eyes, and my eyes closed; she placed her hand on my forehead and I fell into a profound and blissful sleep. Where was I taken? I don't know. It was doubtless to a distant house, hidden by the trees and thick bushes of a vast abandoned garden, where I was left with the sole company of my visions. Perhaps, one day, I'll relate them to you, and you can tell me whether they're concordant with the events that agitated the world during that century.

"Yesterday, my solitude was troubled by frightful nois-es; terrible nightmares tormented my lethargy, I struggled all day in frightful embraces. When midnight came, the panels that formed my chamber broke violently; I sensed the assault of a furious crowd around me. I woke up, and

I saw a man standing by my bed. He was covered in rags; the wrinkles of hunger and despair furrowed his face; his bushy hair and twisted beard were bristling. He was swinging a redoubtable club in his black and chapped hands, and I thought I recognized him, having seen him once before in the tremulous streets.

"He was crying liberty, like those of old; his brethren, like him, were howling that fateful word; they were grunting effortfully, a herd bruised by wounds, a bloody and desperate horde, and, terrified, I fled before them through the park, the ground of which became soft for me and whose thickets favored my flight. I was able to escape their pursuit, and their clamors had scarcely calmed down when you came along.

"But I can still hear them," she said. "Listen! A tumult of weapons is filling the city, bells are ringing, rumors of wrath are audible, they're coming back, and I've only slept to relive the morning of my life. Their cries are drawing nearer; let me return to the peaceful dwelling of dreams and forgetfulness."

With an abrupt gesture, she wrenched herself out of my grasp and disappeared rapidly, while murmurs rose up in the city, murmurs full of amour, dolor and hatred, which rose into the joyful and bloody sunrise.

Testis' voice faded away into a feeble crystalline sonority; a slight frisson ran over the shoulders of the grave men by his side; the flower-garden took on an aspect of antiquity, and at that moment, Juste thought he could see strange and mysterious smiles passing over the lips of the Ceres, the Pomonas and the Floras.

"That man is subversive," he said. "What would become of him if he went to relate his old dream in the squares and at the crossroads?"

"Nothing," someone said. "The people are wise, and if his fate, quite acceptable, isn't perfect, he's able to wait patiently for the inevitable ameliorations."

Everyone nodded their heads with conviction, and yet, the eyes fixed on Testis were anxious. Marcus thought he was seeing an assembly of the faithful united around an old fetish, whose role was to awaken fears in the souls of those who came from time to time to listen to the oracle.

Silence fell again; the members of the audience, without speaking, looked again at the decrepit idol, and then stood up one by one, and after having bowed, went away along the pathway hedged with trimmed box-trees. Only one of them remained, a little man with rickety and tremulous legs, lingering in his contemplation. An abrupt and sudden burst of laughter woke him up; he cast a frightened glance at the person who had announced his advent thus, and departed precipitately.

"Did you see them. Claude?" asked the laugher.

"Is that you, Anselme?" exclaimed Claude, and, turning to Marcus and Juste, he introduced him to them. "The last poet in Geronta," he said. "I've mentioned him to you." And, addressing Anselme: "I've told my friends about you."

"You've directed them in their pilgrimage," said Anselme. "How did you find our old Testis?"

"Very ugly," said Juste, "but I knew him already, and my opinion has little weight. It's for Marcus to speak."

"My good Juste, Testis doesn't interest me. What he can evoke, I know better than he does, and the prophetic form he gives to the present can't seduce me. He might open young souls—Claude is an example, and perhaps the only one—but he's impotent to bring me the slightest idea. He excites my curiosity, as an ancient relic would, some debris of a lost planet or a specimen of an extinct species. If he didn't talk, he'd be as precious as the skeleton of a mammoth or the imprint of a fern in a lump of coal; I might depart from him to build an entire world; he might be the pivot around which my thought would turn. But he talks, both too much and too little."

"I understand what you're saying," Anselme replied, "and yet I don't share your sentiments. I like Testis. I like his voice, like the sound of an antique instrument, and I like the sad and ingenuous charm of his story. That awakening of the princess in the nascent dawn pleases me, and not only because it excites fear in the obtuse brains of those who you saw fleeing just now. For me, Testis is the knight of that infantile Aurora who resolved to live in the dwelling of dream and forgetfulness. What a sweet dream! To go to sleep one tempestuous morning and to wake up to a peaceful evening!"

"Yes, the dream of a naïve egotist," said the philosopher. "The dream of a cowardly heart and a poltroon spirit, the dream of a feeble soul desirous of profiting without difficulty, without dolor and without anxiety, from the terrible labor of others. How ugly it is when one strips away the faded and sentimental frippery with which poetry tries to dress it! Does not the master asleep in the fields while the army of his slaves toils, waking up when the sun sets, after the harvest is brought in, realize it every day? Is that truly the desire of your life, Anselme?”

“I haven’t yet arrived at that degree of wisdom, and I’m pursuing something other than I shall doubtless attain.”

“What?”

“You have the custom of talking in parables, Marcus; let me imitate you and tell you the legend in which my desire is hidden.”

They had quit the grotto in which Testis had gone back to sleep, and they were sitting on the grass of a solitary lawn, which the declining sun dappled with bright patches.

Anselme spoke.

XVII

The Last Siren

THERE was once a castle built on the edge of the sea on the Mediterranean coast. It stood on sheer white rocks, and one of its faces gazed perpetually at the waves, through the profound blue irises of which marine plants caused dark flashes to pass. As the forest died out at the edge of the strand, the tall and elegant pines shaded the turrets with their parasols, and their somber verdure veiled the manor with melancholy, which only smiled over the waves; thus, the dwelling had a double aspect, and that duplicity augmented the mystery with which the terror of the fishermen had surrounded it. When the wind blew—and in that region its violence was abominable—the pines, bent over by the tempest, seemed to want to hug the walls; their needles rattled, and frightful harmonies were heard beneath the foliage.

On the side of the cliff, a door was pierced in the wall of the castle, from which a stairway descended toward the waves, as if to await the gilded galley of a princess who would arrive one day. The water was tumultuous against the granite; one divined profound fissures hollowed out under the reefs, vast grottoes in which gods were perhaps asleep.

The manor had been deserted for many years. The ivy had caused the battens of the doors to yield beneath its embrace; it had dislocated the stones and broken the steps of the seigneurial perron. Along the pathways in the gardens and the orchards, the carpet of fallen leaves had thickened in the solitude, and it extended its smooth bronze sheet, which no human foot had ever soiled. Giant rose-bushes, iron virgins, had raised their hedges around orange and lemon trees, and jasmine bushes leaned on the trunks of almond trees.

The castle was protected by legend and dread. It had once been inhabited by a noble and ancient family, and the local mariners and peasants related a troubling story about the hereditary lords. According to them, no one had ever seen the eldest sons of the Barons de Torsis, as they were called, succeed their fathers, thus inheriting the titles and privileges of the house. The heirs of the Torsis were always younger sons, and the eldest always perished in a similar fashion. When they reached twenty years of age, they were found, one morning in May, lying on the steps of the stairway leading down to the sea. They bore no wound; no spasm had twisted their limbs or convulsed their face; they seemed to be asleep in death, the eyes partly open, shining and ecstatic, the arms curved inwards as if in a grip, but on the mouth was a bloodstain, like the bite of a kiss.

One day, the Torsis had abandoned their manor, fleeing before destiny. They had closed the doors of that tomb, and since then, none of them had returned, even to honor the memory of the dead Torsis who reposed beneath the marble slabs, under the eternal vigil of the baying waves, which beat the walls of the crypt with their silver helmets. Since then they had lived at the court; some had distinguished themselves in embassies, one as a minister, others had become illustrious in the camps; there was even a renowned general among them.

After their departure from the castle, fate had been favorable to them, and the eldest sons of the Torsis had been able to perpetuate their race. Nevertheless, one of them still perished mysteriously. He was a mariner, and one evening when he was returning from the lands of the Orient his ship stopped before the family dwelling, which appeared to him in the distance, bloody in the sunset. His companions related afterwards that at the sight of the disquieting turrets, a shadow of melancholy had paled the forehead of that Torsis. He had leaned on the rail and contemplated for a long time the pines inflamed by the sunlight; then, when night fell, he sat down in the poop and asked to be left alone. He was obeyed, and when dawn came it was seen that he was still sitting on his bench; his crimsoned lips let no breath pass; he was dead. Thus, once again, the younger son of the family inherited the title, but he was the last to cause the lineage to deviate.

Centuries of abandonment had passed over the castle when it reawakened to life. One spring day, the fishermen saw the house invaded; crews of workmen had come from the city to trouble the silence of the marvelous gardens and the peace of the vast halls. The rose-bushes, the ivy and the jasmine were mutilated by adroit gardeners; the steps of the disrupted perron were consolidated; the pines that held the walls prisoner with the network of their branches were driven back, and fresh air traversed the neglected chambers, the corroded drapes of which fell apart in the saline air.

When the castle was furnished, and the park and orchard had resumed their beautiful order, the master arrived. He arrived at dusk, and his horses could barely fray a passage through the surprised crowd that gathered to see the frail and sad young man who had returned to the seat of his ancestors. He was the last of the Barons de Torsis; at twenty years of age he remained alone, having never had a sister or a brother, and his father and mother having died, undermined by the malaise that attacks old lineages to excess.

When René de Torsis crossed the threshold, those who had accompanied him thus far sensed a vague anguish grip them, for, as the sun disappeared over the horizon, a trail of blood ran over the waves and came to attain the last step of the legendary stairway that faced the sea. Only René did not tremble, and a sort of joy illuminated his face as he entered the vestibule ornamented with mosaics.

He had a light collation served; after having eaten he sent away his domestics and penetrated the bedroom that he had chosen, one of those whose windows overlooked the water. He cast a distracted glance over the tapestries and the furniture, nodded his head, as if the décor pleased him, and then came to lean on the balustrade, looked down at the rocks, and lost himself in a dream.

He had lived alone until his twentieth year, pursuing sad dreams during his youth and adolescence. He had been born deprived of everything, and had been ignorant of joys as of dolors, his existence having been one long torment. He had never experienced anything but a heavy lassitude; he bore on his feeble shoulders the burden of ages past, and at the moment when he knew a desire it was the desire for death, mingled with a desire for amour. Women were, however, indifferent to him; his eyes had not opened to their beauty, and it was vague phantoms that trouble his sleep. An imprecise, mysterious sentiment invaded him, however; he felt summoned. He knew the history of his family; old servants had related it to him and he had often shivered in his childhood at the repeated tale.

As he had grown older, a preoccupation with those somber adventures had developed, but gradually, he had forgotten the details; only one had subsisted, the obsession of which increased with the years and oppressed him entirely. Soon, he only thought of one thing: the mouths of the corpses, each mouth bloodied by a kiss, terrible but so sweet that it killed. One day, he could no longer resist the attraction of death; he decided to return to the castle that gave forgetfulness, and he departed, going toward his bride.

He thought about all that while darkness fell. In the distance, the moon paled the waves; he watched the star rise, and while it shed its blond light, he listened to the floating harmonies. Little by little, they became more precise, accumulating, and he heard a voice.

What was it saying? Doubtless he understood the strange words, for he got up abruptly, traversed the dormant corridors, arrived at the low door that opened on to the cliff, opened it without hesitation and remained motionless on the threshold.

The voice reached him more distinctively and more seductively. It was the summons. Radiant with jubilation and tenderness, he set foot on the top step of the stairway leading down to the sea and, as he was about to descend, he saw her. She emerged from the white wave, lifting her golden hair with her alabaster arms, spilling marine peals over her breast. She continued singing without looking at him.

Suddenly, she raised her eyes toward him: green eyes, abyssal eyes.

He held out his arms and said: "Here I am."

"Here I am," she replied. "I was expecting you."

As if he were obeying an order, René lay down on the steps, and she went on: "You had to come and I had to see you. Without you, life was weighing upon me. Alas, it has been too long, my life, since the day when, on the Erythrean Sea, the frightful voice cried the death of Pan. I have survived my sisters, and here, in the Neptunian grottoes, people have forgotten me. My voice always made itself heard in the meantime, but men were not listening, they did not understand my songs, and my agonizing beauty. Why did those of your race understand my words? Doubtless it was a favor of destiny. I have had the most handsome of your family for lovers, until the dolorous moment when their senses too were veiled and when they fled, forsaking me.

"I have lived in spite of everything, for I hoped for their return. One of them came to seek me one evening, which his flag-decked gallery, and then, abandoned again, I let the hours go by in waiting. You have come, finally, the last of your line, and after you, no one will come. You are the most fortunate of all the Torsis. Your brothers died of my kiss, but tonight, I shall die of yours, while you faint under the caress of the last of the Sirens."

In her turn, she extended her arms toward him; inclining like a flower, he came to fall upon the beloved breast; their lips met, and as the moon came to kiss the granite, the last Torsis and the last Siren expired, enlaced.

✳

Anselme fell silent and looked at Juste. Juste shook his head; he opened his mouth as if he were going to speak, closed it, opened it again, and, after a few seconds of that mute pantomime, he made up his mind.

"Monsieur," he said, "don't be offended by my words, but your Torsis appears to be of the family of our friend the symbolist. He really was a sorry fool, and if I had known him, I would have tried to cure his woe. I know people who have given their lives for the caresses of a woman, but it seems to be going too far to die in the embrace of an amphibious creature, not knowing the pleasure that one is going to seek there."

He stopped at a sign from Claude, and listened to Marcus.

"It's the old song," murmured the philosopher, "the old illusion and the old lure. Beauty once appeared, she reigned in distant ages, and the evil crowd has killed her. She has been reborn, but only the divine poets and artists, the great geniuses, the entire race of privileged lovers, possess the secret of her resurrection. For them, she reserves the softness of her eyes, the kisses of her mouth; they are the initiates, they know the palace she inhabits, and for them she quits her veils. She lives in a rude country to which a harsh and rough road leads, a somber road that few can follow to the end, and into which the elect only enter after having lit the torch of the suns of old . . .

"And all of that is untrue. Forms change but beauty remains, for beauty is life. Those who cannot see it around them are the embalmers of cadavers, the illuminators of mummies. What death are you seeking, then, Anselme? What defunct chimera are you pursuing? Why attempt to attain a shadow and not a living ideal that you create in pursuing it? Vivify your desire, open your eyes to the world; you will see beauty, and beauty will be within you, if you sense it externally."

"It is within me," said Anselme.

"Yes, within you, as a virgin in a shroud is in a tomb. You ornament it with jewels and lace, you perfume it with penetrating essences and you forget to live in contemplating it, you forget that the sun shines, that the sap stirs in the bosom of the earth than that the Anadyomene surges every day from the foam of the sea."

Anselme bowed his head and his distracted hand tore up grass, one blade at a time, and threw it behind him.

Marcus continued: "Is that where you have put all your strength and all your energy? Opening sepulchers, exploring necropolises, and trying to stifle the present under their dust! Plunging into catacombs, closing your eyes to the light, and judging the sun ruddy by the pale clarity of bleak antique lamps! Anselme, those who speak in the name of yesterday speak in the name of death."

"Is it necessary, then, to scorn the past, to hate the work of the ancestors?"

"No, but it is necessary to continue it and not to wallow in it. Think about those who were the workers of old, those whose spirit palpitates in the stones of our edifices, in the constructions of our philosophies and our ethics, but don't seek to imitate what they did. Why always dig the same field when the great heaths of infinity are open before you? . . . You're not replying? I'll speak your language, then, and ornament with the veils you love the verity that I want to teach you."

And the philosopher, having meditated momentarily, spoke to Anselme, while Juste and Claude listened.

XVIII

The Past

NICOS lived in Tarente when Tarente had not subjected to the assault of the Roman she-wolf. He was a poet, and, although he was young, the rich often invited him to their tables, where he entertained them with his epigrams. That was the sole profit that he obtained from his poetry, but it was sufficient for him, insofar as he was content to eat once a day.

His existence was uniform; he wandered in the morning through the outlying districts of the city, where wool was dyed crimson and skillful artisans wove transparent fabrics with the silk of mollusks. Sometimes, he went to walk along the banks of the Galese; he sat down in the shade of pines or lindens, and, depending on the season he went back to Tarente with his arms laden with lilies, verbena or poppies. In the afternoon he did not leave the Acropolis. He took pleasure in contemplating the fishers of oysters and mussels who haunted the little marine lake, and especially the Choerades lying in the milky sea, islands protecting from tempest and winds.[1] When the sun's glare

---

1 The Choerade islands in the Ionian Sea are mentioned by Thucydides, although other Choerades in the Euxine Sea are cited by Theocritus.

eased, he went to listen to the words of old Philas, his master and friend.

However, that happy life, which many sages would have envied him, did not always satisfy Nicos. When he reached twenty years of age, he became ambitious. He dreamed of making long and beautiful poems that would give him the glory of a great aede. He resolved to sing the praises of the triumphs of the demigods of old, for he was somewhat scornful of those who depicted the mores of artisans and took pleasure in celebrating the present time—which, as everyone knows, is a parody of antiquity. He decided to leave Tarente and, one morning, Philas received a poem of adieu from him. That poem would have been mysterious for those who were not initiates, but it was clear to the philosopher. It said:

You will find, to the left of the dwelling of Hades, a lake beside which stands a white cypress. Avoid approaching that spring. But you will find a second further on, which emerges from the Lake of Mnemosyne and pours out fresh water. Guardians are beside it. Say to them: "It is a child of the Earth and the starry Heavens that is entering. I come in supplication, as you know, O celestial race, with a thirst of which I am dying. Give me then, as soon as possible, the fresh water that flows from the Lake of Mnemosyne, in order that I might drink and appease the ardor of the divine thirst." And then they will enable you to reign among the heroes.

Philas understood that his pupil was going to visit the land of the gods, to seek myths and symbols in the sacred fountains, and to attempt to equal the greatest of rhapsodists. He hoped to live until he returned, in order to greet him when his feet touched the soil of the city.

A few years went by. With the passing of time, old age curbed Philas' shoulders under its heavy burden, and he despaired of seeing again the youth he had cherished like a son. He envied his fate and the joy that he would experience in marching in legendary fallow fields on the banks of sacred rivers, through meadows that had quivered with amour under the feet of goddesses. He would have liked Nicos to bring to his old age a little of the perfume on the lentisks and olive groves of Hellas.

One evening in autumn, in the epoch when great gray wings seem sometimes to pass over the mirror of the sea, whose blue pales, Nicos came into Philas' house. He had become as robust as an athlete, his skin was tanned and his eyes, once dreamy, were now sharper and bolder. He was not alone; a woman accompanied him, whose beauty made the old philosopher incline his head: a brunette woman with russet eyes, so large that they seemed to want to come together, a woman with a complexion gilded by distant suns.

When Philas, weeping with joy, had hugged his friend, and had paid his companion the just tribute of admiration that was due to her, he interrogated the traveler. He asked him whether, out there, near the antique springs, he had commenced the work that would immortalize his name.

"I have not made songs, Philas, nor poems; I have done better," said Nicos.

"What, then?" asked Philas.

"I have loved, since I have seen the world, and nothing that was not the present was able to distract me. I have encountered my friend; she has saved me from the icy grip of antiquity. Nothing is more beautiful than life, Philas, but it is necessary to live it, and not to attach oneself to the dead. I have renounced singing the praises of yesterday, but, alas, what can I tell you, my master? I am sad, and she is sad. We savor the present moment, but it still appears to us to be cold; vague regrets haunt us, we fear that we have offended the souls of the ancestors who live around us. That is why we have come to you, to ask for help in our distress and to beg you to show us the way."

"You are a child, Nicos," Philas replied. "You have lived in the past for a long time, and when you encountered the divine today, you were afraid of the friend of former hours; you saw his complexion pale, his forehead grave; you fled, and carried with you in your flight the regret of separating from him. How vain is your fear! Listen to me, my son, and you will be consoled.

"It is not necessary to believe, Nicos, that yesterday is dead because the sand in the hour-glass has marked its fall. Yesterday lives within us; it is our substance, and it is thanks to it that we can savor the splendor of the moment. Do not disdain what you once cherished, love it more; do not adore it like a defunct god, seek to comprehend it. The past gives grandeur to the present, and it is via the past that we attach ourselves to the obscure future. It is the dead who light our way, the dead disdainful of servile men and benevolent to those who know how to listen to them. Do not scorn the dead who hold the torch.

At this point Philas drew away; he opened his door very wide, and the lovers saw the sea, draped with its veils and its crepes. The old man showed them the waves, and went on:

"If you don't believe what I say, go down there to the strand, and, without worrying about the vain seashells of which your feet are making dust, and which only children take pleasure in collecting, listen to the great mistress; her crepuscular and matinal rumors, voices age-old and still young, will enable you to understand that life is nourished on death. Do you remember, Nicos, the legend of Tegeates? Let me tell it to you again. It recounts that the rich Ares was united one day with the daughter of Cepheus. She died one day in giving birth to a son; that son remained with the body of his mother; he continued to suckle, and the breasts of the dead woman nourished him with an abundant and pure milk. Shall I explain to you what is meant by Tegeates?"[1]

"No, Philas," replied Nicos. "I've understood that the past, although dead, can still nourish us with an uncorrupted milk. We're going to remain with you, if you wish. I shall sing the soul of the living, the sister of the soul of the dead, and in the evening I shall recite my poems, poems of today, sons of those of old."

"Fathers of those of tomorrow, Nicos! For that is the truth! You have attempted to embalm the past and you have seen the vanity of it; you have isolated the present and you have felt sad; so do not make it immobile, and gaze through it at the future . . ."

"I understand too, Marcus," interrupted Anselme, abruptly. "It's necessary to take the eternal river at its source, following the flow, and scorning the infecund sands that it leaves on its banks. There is no past, there is no present; there is life without commencement and without end. But

---

1 The son of Ares and Aerope, the daughter of Cepheus, who was nourished on his dead mother's milk, is usually called Aeropus, but the inhabitants of Tegea claimed him as their city's founder, hence the alternative name.

where are the immortal waters heading, and if it's necessary to abandon ourselves to them, what stars ought to guide us?"

"I'll show them to you, Anselme."

They had forgotten themselves; night had fallen and they could see the crown of flames by which the city of the poor was encircled. The wind was curbing the tall poplars and agitating the oaks; a cold breeze ran over the lawns and flower-beds; the greenhouses, pavilions and porticoes were drowned in shadow, and the trumpets of the wardens could be heard resounding, the first appeal announcing that the gates were to be closed. They stood up and quit the deserted garden.

Someone was following them; it was Irène.

XIX

Joyful Hearts, Uncertain Souls

IN SPITE of Claude's insistence, Anselme did not want to accept the hospitality he offered him and took his leave of the three companions.

"Until tomorrow," the philosopher said to him.

He did not reply, and drew away at a rapid pace. He was in haste to be alone. He did not go into the low city but went along the river bank. The docks ended at the entrance to the bridge but the quays were prolonged, extending their parapets eastwards. To the left, the foreigners' quarter extended its islets, strictly separated according to nationality, and its common streets were invaded by a host of sailors and cosmopolitan merchants running to the taverns and brothels. It ended at the enclosing fortifications of Geronta itself, and backed up against the first protective wall.

Anselme went through the gates and breathed more freely. After the ditches and the embankments, the plain unfurled its fields of wheat, its enclosures of vines, its orchards and its vegetable gardens, huddled together, groaning with life and potent sap. It was the city's nurse, and an entire population of peasants, curbed over the cultivated ground from dawn to dusk, caused wheat and wine to emerge from the soil. The strong odor coming from the furrows and the trees, whose fruits were beginning to swell, troubled Anselme; he went down to the very edge of the river, which, emerging from its bed of stone, was flowing without hindrance. He sat down on a heap of stones and meditated.

Why had he listened to Claude, and what did that old man matter, whose words he could still hear resounding in echoes within himself? He had arranged his existence a long time ago; he had been able to flee outside life—the life that was so ugly, so empty and so odious to true lovers of the beautiful. He had built for himself a city of dreams, memories, and divine illusions: a white city covered with temples, in each of which a divinity was enthroned; and all those temples surrounded one unique, inaccessible temple, that of beauty, of which each god represented one aspect. He went from altar to altar, carrying his incense and myrrh to all of them, placing himself above the soiled realities, deaf to any voice that was not the voice of the sovereign, full of corn for those who did not know the mystery of the rites, the meaning of the psalmodies.

He had believed that he was safe behind the walls of marble that he had raised himself, ornamented with marvelous friezes, bas-reliefs and statues, the walls that were so high that they hid the world, so thick that they stopped all sounds, the sound of sobs as well as that of coarse laughter, but the speech of a stranger, the sudden evocation of the tumultuous present and the problematic future had sufficed to extract that confession from him a little while ago.

Was the philosopher right? Could nothing be edified on the ashes of the dead, and were the fruits of the past similar to those beautiful desert fruits that contain neither pulp nor juice, but only an insipid dust? Was it the consciousness of that inanity that put in the depths of his heart that perpetual anxiety, the desire for the chimera never attained, hidden in the sanctuary that no one entered, into which he did not want to penetrate for fear of finding it empty, or not encountering the expected image there. What if she did not exist, that immutable goddess? What if it were true that it was necessary slowly to create her, if he had exhausted his strength pursuing a shadow?

The water fled before his eyes, flowing eastwards, toward the sea, whose tide made itself felt all the way here, swelling the bosom of the river slightly. What forms had once leaned over that mirror? He did not know, and he saw that it was his own folly that had attempted to attain the reflection that had fled. However, he had put his joy into that pursuit; that was what had enchanted and ennobled his life. Now someone had just broken the charm, and he sensed that the man was right.

Vessels were passing by; he gazed at those quitting Geronta. What if he were to depart with them, if he were to go beyond the oceans, far away, to some unknown Eden where he could continue his dream, or, perhaps, attain it, one evening, as Torsis had conquered the Siren? Yes, but Torsis believed, and he had reposed happily on the bosom of the one who offered herself, whereas he, if he saw the object of his desire now, in the midst of the waves, he would say to her: "It's not you." He lacked the invisible faith; if he had had it, he would have defied all assaults, whereas he had yielded to the first attack.

A breath of wind reached him. What formidable mouth had exhaled it? It was the breath of the sea and the breath of the river, the breath of the rumbling city and the breath of the fields. It was the bitter perfume of fogs, the warm perfume of aromatic plants, the acrid odor coming from the factories and the greasy odor emerging from the soil; it was the rumor of the waters of the occident and the appeals of the abyss of the orient, the murmur of sleeping beings and the plaint of those who were awake, the harmony of foliage and the song of meadows: the great voices of the wine rolling its swell, submerging the pale phantoms that haunted his heart.

A profound sadness gripped him. The night was dense around him; he experienced a singular sensation. He thought that one of the ships whose masts he could see plunging into the darkness had just left him there, on an unknown shore, and he twisted his fingers and cried out, feeling that he had been abandoned by his former friends and not finding new friends by his side.

Suddenly, however, he felt the caress of an arm around his neck. He turned round and saw a woman next to him.

"What are you doing here," she said, "alone on the river bank? What despair brought you here? Are you suffering? Are you hungry and cold? Come, take my hand and let me guide you."

"Is that you, Irène?" he asked.

She did not seem surprised that he knew her; she came closer still; he felt her supple body against his. She looked at his face.

"I saw you today," she said. "I know who you are, and I've often heard your name pronounced."

She fell silent for a few seconds, and then she leaned forward and murmured, in a low voice: "The old man talked to you too. I met him one evening and my happiness fled; the work of every day seemed vain to me."

"You were living in the present, though."

"Yes, I was bandaging the wounds of others and he said that I was conserving them; I was wiping away tears and he reproached me for perpetuating them; I was consoling people, and he accused me of maintaining evil—and the futility of my work appeared to me. However, it is necessary that I attach myself to those who are suffering, like the ivy to the elm. I saw you alone, I came to you, and I shall go to others. The route the man has offered me frightens me; and it frightens you too. I heard you in the garden, and I heard him, for I haunt the places he haunts."

In his turn, Anselme drew Irène to him and stroked her hair gently. In listening to her, he had sensed his mental tumult easing. The breath that had oppressed him a little while ago he now breathed in, and he was reborn. A light, new for him, illuminated the river, the deserted road and the vast, quivering fields. The clamor of the city resounded like an appeal. He gazed again at the vessels that were departing; a siren bellowed in the darkness, but its nostalgic cry did not move him. He extended his hand toward the somber suburbs dominated by the multicolored flames, and over which the rain of ash and scoria fell.

"The old man is right, Irène," he said. "It's down there that it's necessary to go."

"To do what?" she cried.

"He's the one who will tell us," he replied.

Slowly, he went back along the bank, almost carrying his companion, and they both returned to Geronta.

As they passed under the arch of the large gate, Irène pulled away sharply and disappeared into the darkness. Anselme had not tried to retain her. Alone, he hastened his steps, marching along the docks. On the other side, in the foreigners' quarter, he heard songs and cries, refrains reached him, and the racket of that vulgar debauchery attracted him. He crossed the road and went into the noisy and populous streets.

He was familiar with the varied appearance and the exoticism of the crowd that agitated there, which had pleased him once. This evening he paid no attention to the diversity of the individuals, races, costumes and languages that collided there. He was in search of light and tumult; he wanted to see life.

As he went past a tavern he looked through the open windows distractedly and stopped. He had perceived Juste in the middle of a group. He pushed the door and went in.

"Aha!" cried Juste, on seeing him. "Here's my friend, the fisher of sirens. Is it the dolphin painted on the sign that attracted you? The dolphin is the friend of tritons, and who doesn't know that those chubby-cheeked fellows hang about with sirens? It's necessary to disabuse you, then, for you'll only find little fish fried in oil here, excellent little fish that aid in drinking the bad wine that Corax likes. Do you like little fried fish? For myself, I prefer them to nereids. If you share my opinion, sit down with us."

Anselme confessed that he did not disdain fried fish. He accepted to taste those that were on the table, took a seat and looked at Juste's companions. There were four beardless young men with long hair coifed in pointed astrakhan bonnets and wearing round spectacles. Sitting beside them were Corax and his acolyte, the one-eyed man. Anselme saluted them familiarly.

"Do you know Corax?" asked Juste.

"Who doesn't know Corax?" said the latter. "You'd have done better to ask the poet whether he recognizes Corax."

"Your humility is divine, Corax," Juste affirmed.

"Oh, my friend, how little I like that word. In employing it as you just did, you seem to be saying that it isn't a human virtue. A singular animal, man; he thinks himself capable of producing all the vices, but he attributes his qualities to celestial intervention, or makes them pale copies of divine attributes."

"Curious!" exclaimed one of the four young men.

"Curious!" repeated the other three; and each of them brought a notebook out of his pocket, in which he inscribed the remark. Anselme looked at them in surprise.

"I haven't introduced you to these gentlemen yet," said Juste. "They're four students disembarked today who have come to study Gerontan morality and philosophy."

"There is no Gerontan morality and philosophy," declared the one-eyed man. "There's only one philosopher and one moralist in Geronta, and that's Corax."

"The one-eyed man is right," cried Juste, "and these young fellows are lucky, on entering the city, to have encountered that new Socrates."

"Corax, Socratic philosopher," yapped a student.

"Socratic," repeated the others, and the sound of pencils on paper was heard.

"What do you think of God, Master?" said the first to have spoken.

"I don't have the habit, young man, of thinking about the unintelligible," Corax replied.

"Oho!" modulated the students, in chorus; and the second among them said: "What is your opinion of morality?"

"I have several—as many as there are moralities, but I've only been able to discover as yet what it is to be immoral. What about you—do you have a conception of the divinity?"

"I can't answer you; it's to my friend that the task in question is attributed, for, in accordance with the custom of our homeland, we have divided the work between us; I'm in charge of collecting the ideas of various moralities."

"Do you at least have a moral doctrine?"

"No more than my friend possesses a theory of the nature of God. He aspires to have one, like all of us; but one day, we shall have one, when, having returned to our homeland, we'll have collated our notes and expressed the juice of all the fruits that we've collected on our travels."

"You'll have to communicate that to us," said Juste gravely.

"As to all the masters whose teaching we'll have followed," the students replied—and the first, who was meditating on God, the second, who was building morality, the third, who was scrutinizing human faculties, and the fourth, who was studying the progress of ideas and social laws, inscribed the names Juste and Corax in their notebooks.

"Young men, you are sage," affirmed Corax, "and your minds seem to me to be vigorously forearmed against enthusiasm."

"Antiscientific!" proclaimed the chorus. The psychologist added, in a shrill voice: "Facts! Facts!" and the sociologist approved.

That racket appeared to shock the one-eyed man. He opened his eye wide and addressed the students. "How do you conceive debauchery?" he said.

"We've sampled it in every country," they replied.

"You might not believe, then, that it's always seasoned here with metaphysics."

"Well said, Cyclops," proclaimed Juste. "Corax, let's guide these young men and show them the evil places of Geronta. Tomorrow, I'll take them to my Old Master."

"What Old Master?" asked the young men.

"I'll tell you that on the way. Are you coming, fisher of Sirens?"

"Gladly," said Anselme, who was amused by the students, and he followed Juste, who drew the one-eyed man with him, while Corax guided his new disciples.

XX

Bluebeard

"AND he teaches?" asked the student of morality.

"By means of parables and myths," Juste replied.

"Like Jesus," said the theologian.

"No, like Plato," riposted Anselme.

"Let's go meet him," said the student of psychology.

They had just entered the Garden of Speech, and they were wandering along the pathways in search of Marcus and Claude, who, according to Juste, would have been there all morning. They had left Corax and the one-eyed man at the door of their common lodgings and, impatient to meet the philosopher, the young men had not wanted to wait until the next day to see him.

They had been walking for a few minutes when Anselme exclaimed: "There they are."

Marcus and Claude were standing in the center of a group of adolescents of both sexes, and as the newcomers approached they heard cheerful voices which were saying to the philosopher: "You're old, you must know new tales."

"I don't know any."

"Then tell us ancient fables."

"You know them all."

"It doesn't matter, we'll hear them again."

"What do you want?"

"Donkey-Skin," cried some.

"Bluebeard," demanded others.

"So be it," said Marcus. "I'll tell you the true story of Bluebeard." And, as he caught sight of Anselme and Juste, he smiled before commencing.

✳

A very long time ago, in a country that no historian or cartographer mentions, there was a city dominated by an audacious castle. That castle was built on the summit of a high mountain, and the houses of the city were spread out over the plain, like a flock of sheep under the eye of the shepherd. The city was opulent, being populated by a few patricians and an infinity of slaves, who worked from dawn until dusk.

Among the richest and most arrogant of the lords was the one to whom the dominating manor belonged. He was known as Bluebeard because his beard had sparkling azure reflections. By that it was recognized that his blood was noble and pure, and that no stain blotted his lineage, for the race of serfs was blond-haired and the race of masters had black hair.

Bluebeard was feared by the entire population of laborers; in the evening, when the work had finished, frightful stories were told about him on the threshold of prisons, and those stories were all true, since Bluebeard was the city's supreme judge, the man charged not only with punishing crimes but also with preventing them.

He was, moreover, a vigilant magistrate. He often came down from his castle and visited the workshops and the outlying districts. He pretended to be benevolent and liked chatting with the young men. When he found one that was better looking and more intelligent that the others he took him as his page, and it was said that, of all those who had crossed the threshold of the castle, none had ever returned. Some terrible mystery was suspected behind the walls of the towers.

Now, in one of the most wretched quarters of the city lived an adolescent who was known as Albus, because he surpassed in beauty and whiteness all his brothers in misfortune. He had large bright eyes, his hair was as russet as gold and he was so frail and weak that he had never been able to work. As he was very proud, he did not accept any charity from the lords of the city, contenting himself with the bread offered by his companions. As he was not constrained to turn millstones, curb himself over any métier, live in the entrails of the earth or extract wheat from the soil, Albus devoted his time to thought. He also gathered all the children around him, and knew how to talk to them.

One evening, Albus and Bluebeard met. They talked for a long time, and the next day, after saying goodbye to the old lady who gave him hospitality, Albus went to the castle. His landlady accompanied him as far as the foot of the mountain, weeping. There she begged him to stay with her, reminding him of the names of those who had gone and had never been seen again. Albus replied that he would look for them, and he climbed the steep slope without looking back.

Bluebeard welcomed him like a son; he dressed him in sumptuous clothes and for a fortnight he heaped him with favors and presents. Pampered, surrounded and served, Albus enjoyed everything that he could have desired in his hours of dreams. However, he was never left alone, and he had been given as a mentor an old man, to whose words he pretended to listen, while reflecting on his new life.

At the end of those two weeks, Bluebeard summoned him, and after expressing his amity once again, informed him of his imminent departure

"I'm obliged to leave the manor for two days," he said. "During that time, I want you to take charge of everything; I'd be very grateful to you if you would."

Albus having accepted, Bluebeard confided his keys to him and showed him around the castle. Then, the arrogant lord having given his page license to dispose of everything he added: "Nevertheless, I forbid you strictly, on penalty of experiencing my anger severely, to open the door that is at the end of the long gallery."

After Bluebeard's departure, Albus retired to his apartment and meditated there for a long time. Naturally, he thought about the door in the gallery, and understood very quickly that he would not be happy as long as he did not have the liberty to use the key he possessed. He did not think for an instant of addressing a plea to his master when he returned; that thought would have been odious to him.

So, he left his room and, without hesitation, going through the deserted halls and abandoned corridors, went straight to the forbidden door. He stopped for a moment before it, and abruptly making up his mind, he opened it.

He saw then that it gave access to a gallery larger and longer than the one in which he was standing, and to either side, against the walls, he recognized the cadavers of the pages who had preceded him. That sight did not frighten him. He went past the bloody cohort without his stride faltering, arrived at the far end of the gallery and, having perceived that it had no exit, struck the wall with his fist.

The wall split under the impact and Albus, having stepped through the breach, found himself in a marvelous garden. There, two warriors, the guardians of the park, came running and saluted him.

One of them said: "You are the victor. The first who tried to enter the path that you have traveled fell, struck down on the threshold; the others recoiled on seeing the bodies of the martyrs who had preceded them, for if the master heaps with presents the cowards that have obeyed him and accepted a facile existence, he kills those who have violated his orders. But you have dared to go on to the end; you have disdained the death that you must have thought inevitable; you have conquered the free life. You have divined, no doubt, that it was not sufficient to disobey; you have escaped the antique chains because you did not want to turn back; you are your own master now. Where do you want us to take you?"

Albus remained silent for a few moments, and then said, in a grave voice: "Take me to those who are in distress. I shall be able to show them were the sunlight is."

Scarcely had he pronounced those words than the castle collapsed, with a horrible din; the garden was illuminated by a softer and warmer light, and on the slopes of the mountain Albus perceived the army of his brothers coming toward him.

The philosopher fell silent; he looked at his listeners and saw that the faces of the young girls were disdainful and scornful.

"Would you like me to tell you the story of Donkey-skin now?"

Bursts of laughter responded, and the troop ran away, abandoning the sad story-teller, whose words they had not been able to understand.

"It's not them who will comprehend, Claude," said Marcus.

"Old Master," said Juste, "I'm bringing you listeners who might be your disciples tomorrow. They're pilgrim students who are going through the world harvesting doctrines, from which they will later extract the precious honey of principles. Their minds are studious and they are attentive; they would like to interrogate you and listen to your lessons."

"I don't spout science, Juste, nor morality nor meta-physics, in the fashion of schoolmasters who know how to slice things up, as peasants know how to divide a buck-wheat pancake. Let them not ask me any questions, then; I know what they will be and I have no prepared definitions, ready-made theories or comfortable axioms condensing knowledge and permitting all brains to store it. Let them walk by my side and listen."

"He's not a dialectitian," remarked the student of psychology.

"Nor a dogmatist," said the theologian.

"I thought I understood that he was preaching altru-ism," observed the moralist.

"You're all right," concluded he sociologist; and all four of them recorded their observations. The scraping of pencils was heard. In the meantime, Anselme approached Marcus.

"Do you remember your promise?" he asked.

"Isn't it for you that I've just spoken? Are you not, like Albus, on the threshold of a new life; will you be satisfied with the fugitive vision of an unknown world, or will you go on to the end without looking back? Are you *en route* toward the good, or will you remain the auxiliary of evil?"

"I've never been its auxiliary."

"What have you done against it?"

"I've avoided it."

"Is that sufficient for you?"

"Why shouldn't it be sufficient for me?"

"Listen."

While talking, they had arrived at the extremity of the island. It was terminated by a vast terrace overlooking the waves, in the middle of which stood a kind of round temple whose roof was supported by marble columns. From there one could see the yellow waters of the river flowing, irrigating the fecund plain, furrowed by the ships that were leaving Geronta. There were islets in the middle, on which lighthouses had been built with red-painted pillars; the waves raised by the ebb and flow came to beat the rocks strewn along the shores, and swirls of foam formed in places. But Marcus' followers paid no attention to the singing waves or to the shifting spectacle of the vessels ornamented by their sails.

The philosopher had sat down; they sat down with him, and he commenced.

XXI

Renunciation

In the remotest corner of the forest of the Ardennes, a man once lived in solitude, unknown to everyone. He had built his cabin far from the noise of cities, in the center of a pretty clearing surrounded by a dense oak wood, and he spent his days wandering beneath the large trees or cultivating a narrow field near his hut, which gave him the vegetables on which he nourished himself, for he abstained from meat, not as a penitence but because he loved the beasts of the woods.

He was mild-mannered and thoughtful; often, when he was digging the soil, he stopped to reflect, leaning on a tree, and the sound of the wind running through the foliage lulled his reveries. When evening came he sought in the thickets a few phantoms that he liked to encounter. Many a time, he imagined that he was alone in the world, and he experienced a great delight in thinking that the clear springs, the beautiful flowers blooming in the sunlight, and the songs of the birds in the treetops only existed for his benefit.

The very monotony of his existence was agreeable to him. He had suppressed effort. In summer, when he was somnolent in the warm hours, all the murmurs of the woodland and the air, confounded in a single chant, penetrated him with bliss. He thought he was hearing the uniform trickle of the sand in a great hour-glass, and he watched the minutes of his life falling, drop by drop.

Years passed thus; his hair turned gray; wrinkles were already beginning to mark his face, and he no longer remembered ever having known a human being. One evening, however, when he returned to his little house, he saw a woman sitting on his threshold. He was gripped by a strange emotion; a tremor seized him, and he ran toward her. Then he stopped abruptly, in order to look at her.

She was a very old pauper clad in miserable rags, covered in thick dust. Her bare feet were deformed and bloody; she seemed to be exhausted; a short, hasty breath caused her breast to bound, and her face was so pale that the solitary could see that she was about to die.

He lifted her in his arms. Her frail body was as light as that of a small child, so he carried it without difficulty to his bed of leaves; gripped by pity, he covered her with his blanket, while she thanked him with a gesture. He sat down beside the bed and waited. She remained thus, without moving, for an hour, her eyes fixed and somewhat vague, attentive, as if she were listening to the advent of night.

When she could no longer distinguish anything outside, not even the confused mass of the trees, she touched her guardian's shoulder with her finger and said: "Who are you?"

"Someone seduced by exile," he replied, "and who has conquered repose."

"Fortunate man," she replied. "Fortunate man, who can close his soul to all dolors and all joys. Fortunate man"—and here the man thought there was a hint of irony—"who can be indifferent to the jubilations of others, as to their suffering."

"I haven't always been thus," retorted the solitary.

"Ah!" she said. "You've been a man with a sensible heart. What was your life?"

He reflected for a moment, inclining his head, listening to distant and forgotten voices, seeing the indecisive procession of past days surging from the profound darkness of the forest, the image of which gradually became more precise, magnified by the appeal of the dying woman, and became so obsessive that he began narrating without any preamble, in a jerky, curt and dolorous tone.

"I had just reached the age of twenty," he said, "and until then I had been confined to the family home, an orphan delivered to governesses, tutors and mentors, never going out except to parade my nostalgia and my sadness through the paths of the park enclosed by high walls. I knew that I was rich. An entire horde of valets and parasites watched over me, the craziest of fantasies were permitted to me, and I was protected from everything except ennui: cruel, pitiless and invincible ennui. Desires haunted me. I wanted to see the world, and behind the high walls I imagined it to be marvelous and radiant, a bearer of unknown delights, triumphant and joyful for all.

"One morning, taking advantage of the slumber of my masters and servants, I went through the sleeping manor, the garden quivering in the early morning breeze and, crossing the barriers, I found myself on the road. Dazzled, tremulous at being free, I went straight ahead, leaping ditches, trampling the heather, letting my gaze run over the boundless horizon, and only a murmur of voices stopped me in my tracks.

"Curbed over the ground, moaning and already sweating when the sun had scarcely risen to the zenith, individuals with bronzed skin, a heavy step, deformed spines and horny hands were digging the soil and striving effortfully without being able to pierce a furrow.

"'What are you doing?' I asked them.

"They looked up; I saw them suddenly become humble and sad, and one of them, an old man, replied: 'We're tilling your field, Master.'

"'Is this field mine, then?'

"'Certainly, since it was your father's.'

"I reflected for a moment, and then said: 'Why are you tilling my field?'

"'In order that you can live, Master,' said the old man.

"'Why aren't you tilling yours?

"'We have no fields,' they said, all together—and it was like a sad dirge.

"'How can you live, then?'

"'We are served the scraps from your table, Master, and we live thus.'

"I fell silent; I saluted them with my hand, and I went back to the manor. The next day, I returned. As on the day before, the men were there, still moaning, still striving.

"'The work isn't finished, then?' I said to them.

"'The work is never finished,' the old man replied. 'Your field is vast, Master, and it's necessary to return to it often in order for it to produce.'

"'Why don't you quit that hard labor?' I asked.

"'We quit it with life,' said the old man, in a melancholy tone. 'But is it not necessary to eat while awaiting death? Those who don't till the earth don't eat.'

"'Make room for me beside you,' I replied, full of good will, 'for I ought to labor too.'

"One of the poor fellows passed me his mattock, and for long hours I made the iron ring against stones. Then, exhausted by fatigue, I went home. The next day, at dawn, I was there again.

"'I've come to work with you again,' I said. 'I want to be your equal, and only stop at dusk.'

"The old man shook his head. 'You won't be our equal,' he said. 'When night comes and the work is done, out there in your palace you'll find a valet who will sponge your sweat, he'll give you clean and perfumed underwear, you'll sit down at an abundant table and you'll retain a memory of the hard day that will die away as your overstimulated appetite is appeased. Meanwhile, in our hovels, beside the hearth that is scarcely blazing, we'll crouch down to eat the hard bread that is our lot.'

"I made no reply; I seized a spade, followed them, and accomplished the labor like them. When the evening bells rang, they picked up their tools, and as they were about to retire I retained them and took them with me. They went into the vast courtyard of my dwelling, climbed the marble perron and went into the vestibule, where lackeys were lined up. Their weary feet were washed, they were dressed in fine and supple garments, and then they were taken into the room where I was waiting for them, for the evening meal. When they had eaten and drunk, they were made to lie down on soft and profound beds. At first light, they got up, and I accompanied them to the fields.

"'We received the same salary yesterday,' I said to the old man. 'Have I not been equitable?'

"'You're full of good will,' he replied, 'and you've granted us, generously, what you believed that you didn't owe us. You've made us a gift, and now you want our thanks, but what can we give you in return, since all the minutes of our lives are yours? Are you asking for our gratitude? Yesterday evening, alas, we saw that your dogs are better nourished than our children.'

"'Am I not a good master, though?'

"'There are no good masters,' the old man declared. 'There are only masters.'

"Then a veil tore before me; I understood that by possessing, I was perpetuating the evil. I blushed to be nourishing thus, to my own profit, the human herd, and I saw the extent to which my charity was illicit and cruel, since it had only served to show those poor men how profound their abasement and distress was. I could not hold back my sobs. I embraced the old man who had revealed the truth to me tenderly and I left, fleeing my house and my gardens, my orchards and my woods, being thirsty for poverty, hungry for renunciation. I arrived here one day; the place seemed remote and peaceful to me; I build my cabin here and I alone labor the field here, on which I alone live."

The moribund woman had listened silently to the solitary. When he fell silent, she leaned toward him and she asked him: "Are you content with your life?"

At that question, the man started to weep, and could not respond, for he had just perceived that he was not happy and that something was lacking in his wellbeing.

"You're only a poor fellow," the unknown woman said, "but you're afraid of evil. One day, it appeared to you, hideous and so abominable that you no longer wanted to live on its products. You fled before it; you thought that it was sufficient to avoid it, and thus you knew egotistical joys; you escaped disaster, despair and sadness, but you did not think that others were subjected to them. Those peasants that you abandoned, perhaps you delivered to the cruelty of your heirs, to the authority of those who sat down in your place, and you had no concern for their destiny. It's good not to enjoy injustice and to draw away from it, but what is that worth if one does not fight it? Do as I have done. If my feet are torn, and if my body is broken, it is because I have wandered the paths and the roads, and, not content with avoiding the evil, or even defeating it, I have tried to realize the good. Have I succeeded? I hope so; if not, at least I have tried. Would you like to take my traveler's staff and go forth tomorrow to continue the work that I have quit?"

The man leaned over the dying woman. He placed his lips on hers, as if to take a little of her soul.

"I'll go," he said, softly.

The woman smiled, as suddenly, without a gasp, she died.

The next day, the solitary buried the person that had brought him enlightenment, and then, without turning round to look at the hut where he had lived for such a long time, he went away toward the field that he had abandoned one morning.

✳

"He isn't a partisan of ataraxia," said the student of psychology when the philosopher had finished his story.

"He's right," replied the moralist. "The meaning of his apologue is doubtless that it's wrong to flee social duty."

"All well and good," objected the sociologist, "but isn't that duty sometimes to resign oneself?"

"You heard," said Anselme. "Why has that man said what I was thinking?"

"Because he lives on prejudices similar to yours, because he does not know justice and does not want to know it. As he likes order, he believes himself to be obliged to found it on resignation, on the acceptance of evil, on the sacrifice of individuals to principles, codes, religions and the host of idols that they did not create, but which they nevertheless worship."

"That's not impossible," retorted the sociologist. "Let's talk about resignation, then."

"Gladly. Listen, Anselme."

XXII

Resignation

AS was his custom, old Jacques had got up that day at dawn. He had picked up his spade and, in spite of the wind and the cold, he had returned to his field. When the sun had set and the wind blew more bitterly and more piquantly, he felt weary. His numb hand could no longer sustain the implement; he let it fall to the ground; then, summoning up his remaining strength, he dragged himself to his hut and, as night was enveloping the fields, he collapsed on his threshold, while a gust of wind shook the rotten roof.

Plunged in that profound lethargy, the forerunner of death, Jacques had a dream, the last of those that haunted him. He saw himself transported into a land of opulence, into a country florid with large and perfumed blooms, laden with heavy crops, embalmed by orchards whose trees were buckling under the weight of fruits. He found himself light and joyful there, content with life, glad of the wellbeing of things and the gaiety of the people he sensed, dispersed in the crannies, but whom he could not see. In spite of those divined presences, Jacques found himself alone, and he set forth, walking straight ahead, in order to find a companion.

He walked for a long time without fatigue. He traversed soft meadows, radiant gardens and peaceful shady woods. He went past streams with lukewarm and singing waves. He stopped on the edges of lakes whose waters reflected a cloudless sky. It seemed to him that a day went past, and then another, but night did not fall; he thought that he was living in a country of eternal daylight and perpetual wellbeing. He did not experience hunger, thirst or lassitude. If he picked a fruit occasionally and drank a little water, it was because he was tempted by the beauty of the fruit or the limpidity of the water.

At the end of the fourth day, however, he perceived a house to the right of the road that he was following, surrounded by living hedges, adjacent to a clump of oleanders. He suddenly had a desire to rest. He went forward, pushed a frail lattice-work gate and found himself before a marble perron. He climbed it. As he arrived at the top an old man appeared on the last step, bid him welcome and invited him to come in.

He followed the unknown man; he traversed a vestibule decorated with a few statues, which he recognized by virtue of having seen similar ones in the park of the seigneurial manor of his village. Finally, he penetrated into a vast hall, and, his guide having invited him to do so with a gesture, he sat down on a wooden stool. He sat there, still and silent, leaning forward, with his elbow on his knee and his chin supported on his open hand, waiting to be interrogated before speaking.

The old man looked at him sadly, smoothing his long white beard, which was silky and curly, with his fingers, and Jacques was becoming anxious, troubled by the silence and the solitude, when his host asked; "What are you seeking here?"

"Peace," replied old Jacques. "Peace and repose."

"Have you not known them, then, that you desire them so keenly? I thought, however, that your life had been peaceful and calm, and that, attached for many years to the same furrow, you had not known agitation or distress?"

"That's true; I've lived tranquil and resigned."

"Resigned? Tell me your story."

"My story is humble; it has no collisions, no disruptions, and no adventures. You'd be disappointed if I told it to you."

"Have no fear, and satisfy my request."

"So be it. Know, then, that when I was born, my first whimper accompanied my mother's last cry, and it was death that I encountered on my entry into life. I was not pampered by my father; nevertheless, he did not treat me badly and brought me up in abundance. When he died in his turn—I was ten years old—he left me the same share of his heritage as my brothers, to whom he confided me.

"My brothers did not love me; they constrained me to the rudest labors, and did not spare me any more than the numerous domestics that they were accustomed to treating harshly. I loved them, however, and even though I suffered from their indifference, I resigned myself to it without saying a word. They were bitter, avid and ambitious, thirsty for riches, and the fortune of others irritated them, for they were also envious.

"As soon as I had reached adulthood they told me that my father had not left me any parcel of his domains and that I was my duty to work if I did not want to be a burden to them. I knew that they were lying, and I experienced a bitter dolor in consequence, but I also thought how unhappy they would be if I obliged them to render those precious fields. I did not want to trouble their wellbeing, although it was egotistical, and I made them the gift of my wellbeing. I even found a satisfaction in that; I was glad of my sacrifice, I took pleasure in it, and it was with joy that I devoted myself to mediocrity for their sake.

"That was not sufficient for them; they grew weary, one day, of seeing me by their side; my generosity wounded them and my poverty offended their vanity. I resolved, therefore, to take devotion to the end. One morning, I left the familial house and took refuge in a distant and unconsidered village were no one knew me. Having made a few small savings from my wretched wages, I bought a patch of land, built a cottage on it and lived there, forgotten by my brothers, resigned to my fate, glad to have sacrificed myself in order to give them quietude, only fearful of not being able to spare them possible remorse."

Old Jacques fell silent. The old man stood up, took him by the hand and led him back to the road. There he saluted him and said: "I would have liked to grant you the hospitality you request, the peace and repose that you require, but I have such a horror of those of your race that I cannot bear the sight of them. It is your peers who perpetuate evil in the word; it is thanks to them that injustice reigns. It is because you resign yourself to theft, pillage and bad faith, that bad faith, theft and pillage persist.

"You sacrifice yourself for love, you say, perhaps because of cowardice, and you thus allow hatred to subsist; you claim to be making the happiness of one alone, and you are eternalizing misfortune. Go where your feet take you, in this country that is too beautiful for your irresolute, empty, feeble and poor soul. Here, in this house, I receive those who struggle, those who have a horror of sacrifice because they love justice."

Old Jacques suddenly woke up. The cold wind was still blowing, chilling his limbs; his eyes opened wide in the darkness; for one brief moment he divined the misery scattered over the earth; a secret voice told him that he had served wealth and avarice in a cowardly manner; his heart swelled with a dull pain, his features convulsed, and he died.

※

A sob interrupted Marcus. He turned round and saw Irène, who was weeping, crouching at his side. She parted her hands, which were veiling her face, and, looking at him, she murmured: "Would you be like that old man? Would you not take pity on someone who requested the supreme shelter?"

"Poor troubled soul," said the philosopher, drawing Irène toward him. "It's still and only pity that you're requesting, then; will you never know the truth? I love you, and yet your fellows are worse than the Solitary and worse than Jacques. They do not renounce, they sacrifice themselves; they do even more, they preach renunciation, they are the apostles of consolation, those who put dolors to sleep, preach acceptance, non-resistance to evil, consent to suffering. They incarnate the most pernicious form of resignation, the active form, that which recruits proselytes, which leads to the cherishing of tears, to loving anguish, to rejoicing in distress, to deprivation and hunger."

"What would you say to them, then?" asked Anselme, "and what is it necessary for us to say to them when the charm of their dolorous eyes stops us on the road, when the sad crease of their mouth and the pallor of their forehead makes the love of our heart shiver?"

Marcus looked at Anselme and Irène for a long time.

"Come closer to me," he said. "Let my hands play with the young waves of your hair, and listen to the man who wants to enlighten your destiny."

They both drew closer; Juste and Claude admired them, and, surprised, the pilgrim students paused, with their hands raised, forgetting to conserve the words of the philosopher, who spoke.

XXIII

The Appeaser

FÉLIZE'S father had found Lux on the evening of a battle, in the middle of a furrow, where the infant was asleep. He had set him before him on his saddle and had taken him to his castle. Lux was four years old and Félize was three. They grew up together, thinking and dreaming side by side, having tears and smiles in common. The same landscapes and the same sensations affected their senses, their minds were nourished by similar impressions and sentiments, and both of them, raising toward storytelling women the same surprised, attentive and delighted face, heard the old and profound legends that are born in the souls of the poor and errant dreamers.

When they reached the threshold of adolescence, Félize did not want to abandon Lux, to whom a squire narrated savage and brutal adventures of war. Accustomed by nurses' fables of compassionate hermits, benevolent giants and knights who redressed wrongs, she heard stories of blood and carnage with alarm. Sometimes, at the squire's stories, a shiver ran through her and a rapid cloud passed over her gilded eyes, obscuring the pupils; her skin became pale and nacreous when listening to the episode of a city taken by surprise; she saw the flight of the bewildered inhabitants, the houses in flames, the old men murdered and the young women weeping.

At those moments, Lux squeezed Félize's little white hand in his own. Like a bird, Félize lay on her friend's bosom, closed her eyes and went to sleep, while the soldier's voice became muffled and faded to a confused murmur. But Lux did not go to sleep; he interrogated his educator. In the darkest caverns of his memory, memories awoke, which could not move Félize. He had endured similar nights; he had heard the tocsins rings, the sound of arquebus fire, and the clamor of conquerors.

Gradually, a more precise image formed within him of a city, that of an outlying district swarming with poor people, and from the black sea of forgetfulness troubling glimmers surged, illuminating a distant twilight populated with fleeing shadows. He thought he was clinging to a friendly shoulder, he felt himself gripped by a protective arm; then that arm slackened, and he slid endlessly into darkness that thickened its waves around him. Then he looked at the soft face of Félize, who was smiling at him as she woke up.

By way of those tales and epics they divined the world. They learned about the miseries of the poor, the dolors of the weak, and, as people talked to them about the triumph of strength and injustice, they understood that there was a justice. Isolated in the manor, far from life, they wanted to know it; they had an idea of it that was both touching and redoubtable. They saw that, for the greater number, existence was like that of flocks of sheep in the midst of which a few ferocious dogs were bounding, and which were decimated by the butcher, and sometimes the wolf.

Often, as the sun was setting, they both went to sit down on a terrace overlooking the countryside. There, they talked for hours. Lux showed his companion the villages whose thatched roofs could be distinguished, and the shadows of the peasants laboring in the fields. He told her what he believed he had once seen, before being brought into her company. As he spoke, his vision of the past became more precise; he perceived somber back-streets haunted by wan crowds, narrow and obscure dwellings; a flood of atavistic sensations stirred within him; he stammered, unable to explain his disturbance, and if Félize pressed him, he said confusedly that he remembered centuries of misery.

One evening, they understood that they loved one another. They told one another so, and embraced as they had never done before. They were in the garden that extended behind the castle, it was autumn, and at that belated hour, a faint mist shrouded the trees, veiled the horizon and padded the carpet of fallen leaves that no longer crunched under their feet. After their mutual confession and their embrace, they wandered silently.

They saw, marching before them in the pathways, the phantom of the happiness that her words had evoked, and yet an infinite sadness submerged their hearts, for they knew that they would never be able to resign themselves to tasting the egotistical joys of amorous minutes. If they were silent, it was because they dared not admit to one another their reciprocal sentiments, nor that that instant of supreme satisfaction had enabled them to grasp more harshly the suffering of those who were their unknown brethren.

Their eyes met; they shared another long kiss, and Lux said to Félize: "It is necessary for us both to depart tomorrow, my beloved; we cannot enjoy this felicity forgetful of others, which, alas, too many people accept. Our pleasures would be poisoned by the despair of the wretched; I would find the taste of tears on your mouth and you would encounter the bitterness of sobs on my lips. Our souls have been too sensitive to the dolors that float on the breezes of the dawn and those of the dusk. It is my own misfortune and that of my family that brought me to your side; it is the misfortune of all that is separating us. Do you remember the legend our nurse told us, the legend of the three knights and the peasant?"

"I remember it," said Félize.

"Would you like to tell it again?"

"Gladly," Félize replied. "There were three knights coming back from Palestine; they had been captives of the Moors and were returning to their manor. On the edge of a wood they met a woodcutter who was lamenting; he was old and bent, clad in rags, and his feeble hands could hardly hold the ax. The three knights were moved by the sight of his tears; they interrogated him as to the cause of his chagrin. The old man replied that a giant had abducted his daughter; he was demanding, in exchange for her return, that all the trees in his forest should be felled, and the woodcutter was bemoaning his weakness and impotence.

"One of the knights, the youngest, said to his companions: 'Let's stop for a moment and help this old man. We've been prisoners, it's fitting for us to come to the aid of an unfortunate captive.'

"The oldest of the knights replied that he was in haste to see his family, the familiar lands and the ancient dwelling; having said that, he saluted the woodcutter and his curiosity satisfied, he resumed his route.

"The two knights watched him go; then they drew their swords and struck the oaks valiantly. They had already been laboring for several hours when they saw a child coming toward them carrying a cup and a ewer. The child engaged them to rest and refresh themselves. One of the knights accepted, drank deeply of the proffered beverage and lay down on the ground to sleep, but the other, the one who had spoken first, pushed away the cup and the ewer; his task was not finished and he did not want to interrupt his work."

"When the oldest of the knights returned home," said Lux, interrupting the storyteller, "he found his house destroyed and his children gone; the second remained asleep in the forest for a hundred years. During that hundred years the third felled the trees of the forest, for they were innumerable and the wood was endless. He had taken the woodcutter's ax, and the woodcutter watched him.

"When the last day of the hundred years elapsed, the one who was asleep woke up; white-haired and decrepit he resumed the road that led to his castle; his heirs did not want to know him, they laughed at him and he wept. But the valiant one, when the hundredth year ended, stood up rejuvenated, stronger than when he had returned from slavery, and he saw the person he had cherished so much, and who had come to search for him, advancing into the clearing."

"We will do as he did, Lux," said Félize.

"We will do as he did; we shall both labor in the forest of poor people, and wait for the morning when we shall be reunited."

If they had quit one another that night, perhaps forever, Félize and Lux would have experienced such a poignant sadness that they would not dare to inflict it on one another, and they waited until morning to separate. They sat down side by side on a mossy bank at the extremity of the park; as before, Félize placed her head on her friend's breast, went to sleep, and dreamed.

She was walking across an arid plain, the coarse dry grass of which bloodied her feet. Shadows were moving here and there, faint shadows that she heard moaning when she stopped to listen to their plaints. She interrogated them, gently caressing the faces that were raised toward her, saying sweet words to the wretched phantoms who surrounded her; when she had spoken, she brushed their foreheads with her lips, which bent toward the ground again. It could be divined that their faces were still as bleak, that fatigue still folded their limbs and arched their spines, but their sobs and their blasphemies were no longer audible; their arms were no longer extended menacingly and if, exhausted and dying, they sometimes let themselves fall, a glimmer passed through their resigned eyes: the joy of arriving in port.

For years Félize walked in the plain, of which she put the tears to sleep, and which was now covered by the snow of silence. A beacon guided her: the high towers of a distant city loomed on the horizon. She wanted to enter it, for all those who had wiped their eyes on the hem of her dress had told her that thousands of their brethren were agonizing there. A river forbade access to the city, and when she arrived on the bank of that river no boatman presented himself to take her to the other shore. She sensed her lassitude; her soul filled with anguish; the sight of that mute land penetrated her with sadness, and her heart and mind were so empty, such a redoubtable terror assailed her, that she called out to Lux.

At her call, she saw him coming toward her, graver than before but still young; mechanically, she leaned over the waves, and the waves reflected her aged features, her hair already whitened by the years, her wrinkled eyelids and her figure, dejected by compassion. She made a gesture of fright. Lux stopped, showing her the river with his open hand; the waters had swelled, they were now foaming and bloody, rolling interlaced corpses and solitary cadavers bleeding from the breast, whose hair was spread out over the surface.

In the distance, in the city, frightful clamors resounded; the bronze of bells was heard ringing. And the appeal of strident trumpets rose up in the reeds of the riverbank. A boat went past; Lux showed it to Félize, and shouted to her: "Come on! It's there that it's necessary to go; it's those that it's necessary to deliver."

Félize uttered a loud scream of horror and woke up. Day was breaking, a bright autumn day gilded by a mild and benevolent sun. They looked at one another; then Lux hugged his lover one last time, and he left, going toward the east while she headed westwards.

The route the Lux followed on emerging from the castle was suddenly familiar to him; he recognized the trees beside the road. He had passed close to them before, and he told himself that by going in that direction he would see once again the city that he had abandoned one evening, the one that haunted his dreams, the city populated by his own people.

At the first crossroads, he encountered grape-pickers. He followed them, glad to see the baskets filled with grapes, and, being thirsty, he extended his hand toward the clusters; but an old man stopped him.

"What!" said Lux. "You refuse a passer-by whose mouth is dry the fruit that would refresh it! Your harvest is abundant, though, it would not have been diminished by the fraction required to slake my thirst."

"Stranger," replied the old man, "The vines that we tend are not ours, and our grapes are counted."

"Is it not you who labor on them?" asked Lux.

"Certainly! Throughout the year from dawn to nightfall, we turn over the other's soil and our misery causes abundance to emerge therefrom."

"And you consent to that?"

"What do you expect, child?"

Then Lux seized the grapes from the baskets; he offered it to those who toiled and, in a powerful voice he cried to them: "Take and eat, this is yours. The earth that you fertilize is yours; straighten your spines and come with me."

The peasants sighed, shaking their heads. Only two young men took the symbolic grapes from his fingers and, having said goodbye to those who remained, they accompanied the man who had awakened them.

It was thus that Lux, emerging from his dream, was confronted by the real. With his two companions he resumed his route, and for twenty years, he accomplished his task. Everywhere that men were groaning, everywhere that mercenary labor was crushing people, he descended, and everywhere, those who were asleep threw away their tools and chains in order to follow the friend who had opened their eyes.

Finally, one evening, his army found itself before the gates of the desired city: the city of misery and oppression; the city whose proud towers it was necessary to conquer in order to liberate the wretched and possess life.

Lux penetrated into the somber outlying district, the sight of which made his heart beat faster. He had departed from there naked and feeble, fleeing swords and devastating fire; he had returned there bringing the word of deliverance. While his men waited for him outside he went into the black dwellings, the gehennas in which his brethren consented to die, and he commenced the work.

Alas, his voice found few echoes. For those poor fellows a slavish soul had been forged, a weak mind, a cowardly and resigned heart, and Lux soon understood that another voice was combating his own. He interrogated the children and young women, and learned that, twenty years before, a woman had come to those who were suffering. She had appeased furies, wiped away tears, calmed plaints, displayed the consoling light of the afterlife, extinguished vain revolts, abolished pride and hatred, and everyone had allowed themselves to be lulled by the gentle appeaser who knew all the words capable of luring human dolor.

"Come to her, then," an adolescent said to her. "She will quiet your wrath and will give you the hope of future felicities, as she has to us."

Lux took the hand of the adolescent and, his guide having led him to the dwelling of the consoler, he asked him to leave him, and he went in. He saw a woman sitting in the corner of the hearth and recognized her, as she recognized him.

"Félize!" he said.

"Lux!" she replied.

"Would you like to wander through the square and the back-streets as we once wandered through the pathways of the great park?"

She consented. All day they wandered. As the sun was setting they went to sit down on the top of the ramparts. Félize, thinking that she had returned to the evenings of old, leaned her face once again on her friend's breast.

"What are you doing?" Lux said to her. "You have just seen your work, and you have not understood its futility, or how bad it is! Is this the way you have labored in the poor man's forest? You have taught him to bear his burden patiently, but you have not unloaded his shoulders. You have rendered him deaf to the voice that summons him to free himself; you have thickened the blindfold that his oppressors have put over his eyes; you have forged more chains for him. You who have a horror of evil, have served to maintain it, to make those who are subjected to it accept it. Look!"

He showed her his army camped outside the city. "Those I have brought with me thought that they would find brothers here, ready to open the gates to them, and they have before them a herd of serfs that it is necessary to liberate in spite of themselves, a herd whose members, at the appeal of their masters, will defend the bastilles and give their blood for their torturers."

"Listen, Lux," Félize replied. "You will see how destiny is accomplished."

And she told him about the dream that had terrified her slumber in the morning of the departure.

"Oh, gentle creature," said Lux, "why have you lived, why have you gone to realize your dream? Alas, yes, in order to attain the good, in order to make the warm, bright sun shine over all, it is necessary to cross the river with the bloody waves, which carries cadavers, the river whose shores resound with the clamor of the dying. Come with me, darling! I will take you on my horse, as your father once took me, and we shall rest after the battle, when we have conquered happiness for all."

A great shiver shook Félize's body; all her limbs trembled; her pupils dilated; tears rolled over her face, which became paler; she shook her head gently, and pronouncing Lux's name, she expired.

Heartbroken, he leaned over her, mingling his tears with hers; then, as if she were still alive, he spoke to her:

"You're fortunate," he said, "and what could you do on this evening, horrible for you, except die? You have done what your feeble soul and tender pity commanded; although you have appeased those who were suffering, you have never thought of striking the suffering itself. You have acted in accordance with your law. I cherish your calming lips, but in the new city, there would not have been a place for you, and you had to perish on the threshold of the new morn. Fragile little maid, you could not follow me; I shall follow you. Tomorrow, after the battle, I will come to meet you, on the unknown route, and you will receive me, as the other received the good knight."

Lux kissed Félize for a long time; he gazed for a moment at the tall towers of the city, and then he rejoined his impatient army, which was waiting for the signal to attack.

XXIV

Stirred Hearts, Serene Souls

THE VOICE of the philosopher fell back into silence, and nothing could be heard but the scratching of the pilgrim students' pencils. Claude, with his elbows on his knees and his chin resting in the palms of his hands, turned an illuminated face toward his master, Juste was grave, and Anselme was meditative. It was Irène who spoke first.

"It's necessary, then, not to console the suffering?"

"It's necessary to suppress the suffering," replied Anselme.

"When will the day come, then, when it is no more?" she murmured.

"It will come," affirmed Claude.

"And those who are weeping," she continued, "those who are buckling under the weight of the burden, is it necessary to pass alongside them without seeking to relieve them?"

"Aid them to carry their burden," said Marcus. "Don't teach them to accept it."

"What ought one to teach them, then?" asked Anselme.

"Justice," replied the philosopher.

"What is justice?" asked the moralistic student.

"It is the condition of wellbeing ."

"It remains for you to define wellbeing," observed the psychologist.

"Is it not the power to develop one's being? So long as a man cannot blossom freely, so long as he is submissive, so long as one category of individuals absorbs the substance necessary to nourish the others, wellbeing will not exist."

"It will exist for some," remarked the psychologist.

"Not even that! Those of whom you talk, always haunted by the dread of losing the power they exercise, limit their own action by shackling the expansion of those they fear, for whoever binds another charges himself with their chains. Dominators and egotists, they abolish certain faculties in themselves voluntarily, diminishing themselves, and their wellbeing is thus incomplete."

"According to you," the theologian insinuated, "general wellbeing is, in its turn, the condition of individual expansion."

"Is that not evident? Until now, humans have put their satisfaction in possessing more than their neighbors, first in material goods and then in spiritual goods, either in terms of power and authority, or intelligence. That is so true that all peoples, or almost all, have admitted as the supreme penitence that of possessing less—which is to say, the acceptance of poverty, humility and the quest for stupidity. The rich thus maintain two modes of poverty, but having done that, they augment the sum of ugliness, woes and suffering, and are attained by the very plague that they have propagated."

"If I've understood you correctly," the sociologist concluded, "wellbeing will be realized by the exercise of liberty and the enjoyment of equality."

"You are correct; and when humanity has achieved that goal, justice will be realized."

The students rose to their feet; they thanked the philosopher for having consented to expose his doctrine to them and asked him for permission to quit him. They were awaited by Corax.

"We are only in Geronta for a few days," said the moralist, who was the common orator of the troop, "and we don't want to leave without having heard all of those who profess in the peripatetic mode, for that seems to have been the custom of the original masters. As for those who occupy the chairs, we are assured that they only repeat what has been said before. We shall, however, visit the university—but before then, we shall come back in order to ask you to comment for us on a few obscure points of your system."

"It's a great honor that you're doing me," Marcus riposted, and he bowed ironically before the young men, who drew away after saluting him.

"Fortunate are the fathers of such sons," said Juste, as he watched them depart, "and how happy the sons of such fathers will be! What placid and uniform souls, what meticulous and orderly minds! I imagine that their brains are divided into little compartments bearing precise labels. With them, there's no danger that they'll ever put a principle of theology into the file destined for morality, or an apothegm of logic in the psychology drawer. Later, having returned to the family hearth, they'll agitate all the files that their brains contain and arrange them very conveniently. In accordance with the captions they bear, they'll be able to guide themselves in life, and they'll transmit them to their children. As for your discourse, Old Master, they'll put them in the pigeon-hole destined for dreams and paradoxes, in the inferno of the library of their cranium, along with the critical fantasies that amuse them now but that they'll soon hide. What do you think, Marcus?"

"They're odious to me, my friend, and it's not for them that I speak; I know that they'll never be able to understand. I'd rather charge myself with convincing Flavien's auditors, or the disciples of the gentle Aure, and yet . . ."

He did not finish, and forgot himself in contemplating Irène and Anselme. They were going down the marble staircase slowly, as if to flee those surrounding them, silent and doubtless pondering the things that had been said. The old man indicated them to Juste and said: "Let's leave them alone."

He drew his companions away.

Neither Anselme not Irène saw them going. Leaning on the high balustrade that overlooked the river, at the extremity of the terrace, they could have believed they were standing at the prow of a great ship, and they abandoned themselves to the mild charm of the evening.

In the east, the sky was paling by the minute, extending faded violet veils above the distant waves. A slow tide was coming from the sea, whose effluvia they could breathe in. They saw the waters rising, which were now flowing westwards; irritated at being retained by the borders of the island, they were whining and foaming, and rumbling with a noise like a propeller—the propeller of the vessel carrying the lovers. Then, driven back by the tide, the muddy waves brightened and became blue-tinted, mirroring the sails of boats and the rigging of the long barges quitting Geronta.

Anselme saw in that a symbol of his new life. His soul was stirred; he could still hear the philosopher's words resounding in his ears; he turned his eyes toward Irène and saw her so pale and faint that he enlaced her with his arms. She did not resist, but put her head on the shoulder of the man who was sustaining her, and her loose hair covered her face and her cleavage.

"Irène," said Anselme, "what if Lux had not abandoned Félize? What if, supporting one another, they had started marching in the direction of the sunrise, wouldn't each of them have accomplished the work better?"

Irène did not reply; she parted the scattered tresses of her hair and looked at Anselme.

"Irène," he went on, "I love the softness of your eyes."

She extended them gently to his lips, and he kissed the eyelids, which had closed under his breath, for a long time.

"Félize was foolish, Anselme," she said. "I'll go with you."

Anselme shivered with joy. He drew Irène closer to him and murmured, very softly: "Listen."

As on the previous evening, he heard the profound voice resounding, the tumultuous appeal of seeds groaning, the plaint of the woods, the clamor of the fields and that of humans, the rumor of beings and things: the eternal, imperishable voice. Henceforth, he would no longer flee it; he let it penetrate him and it filled him. He grasped its meaning, he would have been able to translate all the dolors and all the joys, all the aspirations and all the dreams, all the despairs and all the hopes. It seized him by the entrails and he surrendered to it. A great wind passed through his heart and expelled the ashes therefrom, as the tide coming from the east carried away the mud of the river.

Irène heard it too, but for her, it was softened and confounded with Anselme's words. She awoke from a dream. Until now she had lived in pity without ever having known tenderness, and now young love had arisen. Unknown desires swelled her bosom, new words rose to her lips; she saw an unknown world opening before her.

They did not say that they loved one another. They listened to one another thinking, in the silence and the solitude. Darkness invaded the orchards and the fields; it came from the horizon, extending like a cloak over the waters, now motionless, which were slowly darkening. An illuminated ship suddenly emerged from the shadows, its ignited beacons brightening the river. They saw their happiness advancing; their lips met and they stammered their two names.

The appeal of the trumpets awoke them from their dream. They perceived that they were alone, and thought about the man who had brought them together.

"Let's go to him," said Irène.

"Let's both go into the city," Anselme replied.

They embraced again, and still enlaced, they set forth. Above the trees that the first kiss of the night was putting to sleep, they saw the diadem of the wretched city floating, and the wind brought them the perfume of the proud hill, mingled with the aroma of spices and the scents of the greenhouses.

The second appeal made itself heard; they hastened their pace and emerged from the darkening park.

XXV

The Disciples

"OLD MASTER," Juste had said on quitting the Garden of Speech, "I'm abandoning you again. I'm similar to the pilgrim students; perhaps, like them, I'm only in Geronta for a few days, and I want to hear Corax's lessons again. If Claude hadn't thrashed him I'd have asked him to come with me, but it would be permissible for him to redeem his violence and he'd be annoyed if I took him away from you."

"You're right, Juste. Salute Corax on my behalf, and ask him not to hold it against me."

"Corax has a fine soul, Claude; he doesn't know rancor, only hatred."

"Have I not merited being hated by him?"

"Have I not said that Corax understands prejudices and is never astonished by their manifestation?"

"It only remains for me to blush in comparing myself to Corax."

"Refrain from doing that; he has a horror of humility."

Claude burst out laughing. Marcus imitated him; Juste's face expanded, and as he had for a principle abandoning his friends when they were joyful, he saluted them with his hand and drew away.

The philosopher watched him go into the foreigners' quarter and disappear; then he said to Claude: "What a good myth one could extract from Juste's conduct! He lives all day in the midst of ideas and returns every evening to plunge into life. It is necessary to follow his example, not in a servile way, for the exclusive frequentation of taverns in which he takes pleasure in insufficient, but it is important never to forget that it is from life itself that new ideas can surge forth."

He took his companion's arm and continued: "Everything artificial there is in this garden wearies me. It appears to me to be populated by shadows, faint and vague beings. I only felt a single breath palpitating here—the one that Anselme brought—and I don't want to come back here any more. What can be done in the midst of flower-beds, bowling greens and hornbeam hedges, in the shade of regular groves of trees, under these pavilions made for rhetors, beside these statues of old gods, whose gestures are fixed?

"This isn't the world that it's necessary to conquer, Claude, it's this world that it's necessary to destroy. Isn't this park the symbol of decrepitude? Just now, in wandering through its pathways, above the respiration of things, I sensed I know not what wind of desolation and death passing. I won't come here again. The children at play don't hear my language, the adolescents don't want to listen to my tales and the old men are frightened by them. I know that my task is finished here. Those I can win over have come to me and the oppression is such in this city that I can't go toward those that I would like to extract from darkness."

They went along a populous streets filled at that hour with a swarming crowd. Along the sidewalks merchants of victuals were stationed, surrounded by hosts of women buying provisions for the evening meal after the day's toil. From down below came the flood of workers emerging from factories, the closure of which was announced by the shrill sound of bells.

The philosopher looked at the people passing by. He thought about the legend of vigorous laborers with powerful muscles and redoubtable strength. Where were those robust individuals? He could have counted those who remained: the carpenters and masons accustomed to working outside, the young puddlers from the foundries, the hammer-wielders and slaughterers from the abattoirs, drowned in the midst of the others, the men with pale or earthen faces, hollow chests, sunken eyes and stooped shoulders: slaves burned by the fire of forges, exhausted by the hot air of furnaces, blanched by poisons, the bone-marrow emptied and the blood impoverished, the brain mutilated.

"They're as weak as those over there," Marcus thought aloud, "and yet it's from them alone that the light can come. They're worn out by pitiless labor, crushed by the machines they operate, but in the depths of their being they have the flower of desire, still alive. They could be enabled to flourish. In those weary bodies, the love of the better, albeit confused and vague, is lurking within them, alive in spite of everything. Awaken them, and their souls will grow. It's necessary to show them that which can exalt their life, extract them from their torpor, increase their dormant will-power. What will their weakness matter then? The time will come when it will be another motor of energy, and on that day they will create individuals."

Under the light of the gas-lamps, which had just been lit, he saw faces faded by fatigue, anemiated by the excess of labor, but on which disgust did not appear. Although some of them bore the coarser marks of dejection, the majority were grave and pensive, and youthful laughter burst from the mouths that the poisoned air of workshops and the emanations of deadly drugs had withered.

"They're children whose limbs have been worn out and their brain oppressed," Marcus went on, "but they're children; the others are old men in whom intelligence is dying. They would perish on sensing the flame of the rising sun, whose glare would vivify these. Understand me, Claude; we aren't thaumaturges, to attempt to awaken those who are lying in the sepulcher, and whom we have only to enable to plunge into putrescence. Let those who are in their death-throes perish, and come into the midst of the living."

"I hear you, friend; it's among them that I'll go to live, and I'll be able to open their eyes as you have opened mine. What you have taught me, I shall teach them; they'll know your words through mine."

"Through ours too," pronounced a grave voice behind them.

"Anselme!" said Claude.

"Irène!" exclaimed Marcus.

"It is two disciples who are coming to you," Anselme declared. "I shall be like Lux."

"I shall not be like Félize," said Irène. "It is with the faith of little Anne that I shall put my hand in his. But I would like to hear you again, since my eyes are finally unclosed and my ears open."

"So be it," said Marcus.

"Here?" asked Claude.

"What does it matter? Perhaps here a seed might remain."

They were outside a tavern. They went in, sat down, and in the midst of the tumult, the philosopher spoke.

XXVI

The Annunciator

IT was a valley of desolation and sadness: a rectangular valley, closed in all directions; a redoubtable and lugubrious prison. On three sides, vertiginous mountains loomed up, the summits of which were so high that they seemed to join up, grim mountains of hard granite on which no tree, flower or blade of grass had ever germinated, but only a dense somber moss in the fissures. As for the fourth side, the narrowest, it was formed by a monstrous edifice made of blocks quarried from the mountains by some Cyclops: a strange, terrifying, indefinable edifice; a sort of apocalyptic beast that was a temple, a conqueror's palace, a fabulous lair of chicanery; simultaneously a court of law, a barracks and a church; an audacious monument composed of subterranean crypts and profound halls, dominated by colossal towers that mounted an assault on the peaks and attained the summits; a terrible nightmare causing its phantoms to weigh upon the souls of the valley's inhabitants.

The valley was inhabited. It was populated by poor, sad beings, paltry and stunted, as pale as flowers deprived of light, for the miserly mountains did not allow a single ray of sunlight to penetrate as far as the sterile ground. So those people lived in an uncertain and vague clarity, in the bosom of a perpetual twilight and a starless night. Their shoulders were stooped, their chests hollow and meager; they had never breathed a pure air and, their hearing having been refined in the solitude, they knew the dolor of hearing the clamor of the winds that passed, howling, above the altitudes. That was the sole rumor that reached them, a mysterious rumor that filled their brains with obscure desires; they sometimes listened to it, sobbing, at the hour when the indecisive gleams that just reached them disappeared, leaving them plunged in the terrifying darkness.

Bleak days went by in that fashion, like faint shadows, and whichever way they turned their pupils, dilated by adaptation, they saw the redoubtable walls. They grazed meager and phantasmal flocks on anemic meadows in which no flowers grew, and, to distract their morosity, they hung little bells around the necks of their lambs and heifers made of silver, a metal common in the age-old rocks; and the valley was filled by a softly shrill and brightly melancholy harmony, which put their dreams, their hopes and their aspirations to sleep.

Among the young men, however, there were some who were gripped by ennui. They were disgusted by the labor of the fields, and they found seeking minerals in the galleries hollowed out in the rock repugnant; they quit the narrow streets of the towns and went to sit outside the high doors, sobbing, demanding through their tears a remedy for their dolor and lassitude.

Now the palace was inhabited, and always had been, by three men who were said to have the key to the mysteries. For countless centuries they had ruled over that land of desolation. The best fruits of the parsimonious soil, the finest livestock and the brightest and most sonorous silver were delivered to them as a tribute. They were considered as protectors, almost as gods. It was said that only their knowledge, their skill and their strength permitted the valley not to be swallowed up, and it was thought that the formidable mass of their dwelling prevented the tumultuous mountains from joining up and crushing the debilitated burgs.

Those men were venerated, respected and feared. Two of them wore sad black robes, the third was pompously clad in red. When they were seen—they did not always show themselves—the first held in his hand a balance with a terrible sharpened beam; the second presented a book which people had the habit of coming to worship, and the third brandished a sword whose steel made the pale people shudder.

When the desperate came to moan outside their door, they spoke in turn.

The first showed them the roads traced in the valley; he told them that no one should quit them, and that faults were weighed in the sacred balance, the just balance, created to maintain order and, in consequence, wellbeing .

The second read them a few passages, which, it was affirmed, had the privilege of consoling; he explained to them that their sadness was pointless and unreasonable, because people had always lived in twilight, that they had been able to love and die there in order to find themselves elsewhere, in a new and empyrean land, a prodigious sunlight, a dazzling clarity that it was necessary to merit. His voice then became softer and more imperative, and he advised the ephebes to go back to the paternal hearth.

As for the man clad in red, he never spoke; he contemplated the young men, nodding his head when some refused to return to their burgs, and bloody corpses were often found near the oak battens: the bodies of the audacious individuals who had tried to scale the towers and whom the red man's sword, the mute blade, had struck.

Centuries passed thus.

One day, in the valley, a rumor spread; an unknown being had appeared, and no one knew where he had come from. He was a tall and handsome adolescent, with a beardless face full of tenderness and energy, with bright blazing eyes and a charming and gripping voice. He had long curly hair; his robust and supple body was enveloped by a white robe tightened at the waist, and his hand was armed with a staff made of an unknown wood. In the evenings he went into houses, sat down by the hearth, accepted the milk that was offered to him, and when people had gathered around him, he talked about an admirable country caressed by embalmed breezes: a garden of sumptuous flowers distilling warm and potent aromas, an enormous orchard with good and tasty fruits ripened by a magnificent star of which the people of the valley only knew the faded reflection.

People listened to the stranger ardently. Soon, all those obscure individuals were no longer content only to hear him at night; they followed him over the bleak meadows, which his words rejuvenated, and the accessible rocks. Their curiosity was insatiable; they never wearied of their guest's stories, and every day, their desire to know the marvelous country became greater. They wanted to know where the embalmed paradise was to be found; they wanted to go to conquer it, and they lifted their debilitated arms, which enthusiasm rendered strong.

The adolescent resisted their pleas for a long time. One morning, when he saw that the ambition of the best had magnified their soul, when he understood that the thirst for something better had enlarged and fortified their hearts, and that they were ready to attempt the supreme conquest, he announced to them that the promised Eden was out there, behind the evil castle, beyond the lugubrious halls and the fabulous towers, and he revealed to them that the three guardians were forbidding entry to the Eden of peace and delight.

Then the crowd uttered a horrible cry, and its members felt a terrible hatred and an intense love germinating within them; an aspiration for wellbeing rose; they cried out for the light and they rushed toward the monstrous edifice. Under the powerful impact, the blocks of stone tottered, the walls split, the battlements crumbled and the terrifying castle collapsed. Under the mass of debris the three dominators were buried; the crowd disdained them, but did not see, either, the handsome annunciator, who was lying on the ground, struck by the last effort of the sword.

The annunciator smiled; he forgave those who had forgotten him and died happy, for the wretched horde whose feet were trampling him was acclaiming liberty, and the flamboyant sun was giving him all of its radiance.

XXVII

Exodus

WHILE MARCUS was speaking, the racket in the tavern gradually calmed down. The drinkers had gathered around the story-teller; they were craning their necks toward him curiously, in order to hear him, and the last to arrive were shoving the first. Their faces were serious and attentive; one might have thought that they were striving to understand an unknown language, and their eyes widened at the tale of the mysterious valley. They also gazed at Irène, whose beauty charmed them, and the presence of such a woman among them surprised them.

"He must be a priest," said one of them, when the philosopher had fallen silent.

"What did he mean?" said a second.

"That's its necessary for us to reach Paradise," affirmed a third.

"Always Paradise," murmured an old man. "Later, no doubt—and in the meantime, misery and hunger."

"Shut up, old man!" cried an adolescent. "Hold your tongue and let those who have no master speak. Do you think that even your salary is superfluous?"

"You're right. In any case, what do words matter, his or ours? Tomorrow, at sunrise, it's necessary to start work again, and I won't be one of those who weep when it's necessary to down tools."

"When?" interrogated the young man,

"When death comes."

"You're too sad, friend," cried a carpenter. "Have a drink, then. That's wiser than listening to fine speeches."

"And appeasers," exclaimed a mason.

"Does anyone know who they are?" asked a puddler.

"The old one looks shifty."

"Perhaps he's one of those who talks in order to make others talk."

"It isn't him who'll give bread to our wives and children if we're kicked out of the workshop."

"The woman looks nice, though."

"I don't like the two who aren't saying anything."

"Why are they silent?"

"Doubtless to listen."

"Let's shut up then."

"I think they're provocateurs."

A rumor ran through the crowd; evil gleams appeared in eyes, hands clenched and a ripple ran through the mass.

"They want to make us say that we're unfortunate," someone insinuated.

"That we're incessantly attached to the work, and that our fate is worse than that of beasts of burden," affirmed another.

"That we give our sweat and blood to our masters," the first went on.

"That we weave silk and dress in rags."

"They want to push us to sing the song."

"The good song!" cried the old man who had spoken before. His stooped frame straightened, and he started singing, while a frisson of fear passed over all the faces. It was a lugubrious melody terminated by a grim cry. It wrung the hearts of Claude and Anselme. Irène's pale face became paler, and the philosopher contemplated those who were listening, and those who had retired to the back of the room in order not to hear.

The song fell heavily in the air; it said:

We're born bowed over the ground,
We're born bent over the task.
  "Don't raise your head, lad."

We're born racked by hunger
We're born bitten by cold.
  "Shut your mouth, lad."

And it's bent over that we live,
And it's bowed down that we die.
  "Silence, lad!"

Who has seen the sun shine?
Who has felt the warm breeze?
  "Shut up, lad!"

But the sun will shine one day,
And the golden wheat will ripen.
  "For whom, lad?"

For those who will come with me,
And whose hearts won't tremble . . .

They had let the singer go on to the end. When he had finished, a cry of terror emerged from all mouths. The trembling adolescent dragged the old man away; a few men followed them; others waved their fists at Marcus and his companions, and they were preparing to attack them when someone stopped them.

"We'd pay too dear," he said.

The flames in the eyes were extinguished, the arms fell back, the faces resumed their bleak indifference; they all went to the long counter that occupied one of the sides of the tavern; the glasses were filled again, and the drinkers scarcely glanced at the philosopher, who went away.

"The seed remains in the ground," he said, when he was on the threshold, "but the soil isn't tilled. That will be your work."

He turned round abruptly. A hand had been placed on his shoulder, and he recognized Corax behind him.

"What do you want with me?" he asked.

"It's necessary for you to leave," the latter replied.

"Leave?"

"Yes—quit Geronta, and without delay, at this very moment. At dawn they're going to raid Claude's house."

"What are they afraid of?" asked Marcus.

"The echo of your voice," Claude replied.

"They're right, but it's too late now; the echo of my voice will remain."

"There's no longer time to talk," said Corax. "Faithful ears collected your words just now. If your work isn't finished, get out of the city. The world is vast and you've done all that you can here. It would be vain work for you to catechize jailers; their souls are inaccessible."

"What about Juste?" said Marcus.

"He's waiting for me," replied Corax. "Take the lead, your friends will take you to the road. Juste will join you at the fourfold crossroads."

"Thank you, Corax; it was written that we'd see one another again."

"It's also written that we won't see one another again. Adieu."

He saluted Marcus with a gesture, went back up the street, and was soon lost in the crowd.

When he had disappeared, Irène took the philosopher's hand and begged him to hurry.

They started walking, heading for the plain. Marcus allowed himself to be guided; he thought about similar evenings, similar flights by night, other departures so hasty that he had left his staff in a corner of a room. He did not protest against his destiny; he had chosen it. Was he not one of those who was never to have a roof, one of those who pass by and sow everyone's field, one of those for whom one house is too narrow, one city too narrow, one fatherland too narrow?

"Who are you?" Juste had asked him on the morning when they met. Today, as before, in the sadness of the exodus, as in the joy of the arrival, he would reply, smiling: "I am the orator of the Truth, the apostle of Justice."

Irène's hand trembled in his; he squeezed it gently. Other hands had also trembled in his; others had attempted to retain him; he had gripped the former and repelled the latter, the dear egotists who wanted to keep him. And he always would, until the day when, worn out by fatigue, he would stop in order to die, after having accomplished his task and prepared the work, the work for which those he left behind him would toil: Irène's sisters, Claude's brothers and Anselme's, the unknown army, the one whose soldiers Corax was instructing.

They traversed the flamboyant city now; they passed in front of the factories whose tall chimneys were vomiting yellow flames, ruddy vapors and luminous sheaves of green and violet. It was there, that army, agitating behind the blackened walls. In the shadows of yards, in the rumbling workshops, in the vast halls, he thought he could hear the old man's song resounding:

> *And it's bent over that we live,*
> *And it's bowed down that we die.*
> *"Silence, lad!"*

Oh, the lugubrious cry of dolor, the terrible clamor of distress, the somber despair of that plaint. Silence, lad! No, not silence, not resignation, but revolt against the evil and against the suffering, the appeal toward the better, toward the good, toward the just, toward wellbeing!

> *But the sun will shine one day,*
> *And the golden wheat will ripen.*
> *"For whom, lad?"*

> *For those who will come with me,*
> *And whose hearts won't tremble . . .*

For those and for everyone, for those who did not know and for those who would conquer life, for the herd whose backbones would be straightened, for the humble as well as the proud, for the strong as well as the weak.

They had just passed through the southern gate; their feet were treading an earth charged with scoria and ashes, a bleak grey earth, still hot, which extended its desolation. Nothing was germinating there, and yet, beneath the infertile surface, the fecund humus was dormant. Untiringly, it was necessary to bring the spade, to dig that infecund soil, to sow the wheat there that the future would harvest.

He had spoken aloud; Anselme and Claude drew nearer, but he fell silent and they dared not interrogate him. They continued to walk silently in the darkness.

Irène was tired, she saw the road stretching before her endlessly; her feet were leaden, her head heavy; her eyes closed and she went on automatically, in a dream, toward an unknown goal.

They were in open country now; to the right extended grassy meadows that descended toward the river; to their left were apple orchards. Living hedges bordering both sides of the road perfumed the air with a slightly bitter odor. The great singing voice of the waters reached them; they heard the rustle of foliage, the confused rumor of the city. The strident cry of a siren cleaved the air; a train fled, rumbling behind the curtain of trees; in the pastures, horses were grazing; a bull bellowed.

A gentle melancholy entered Claude's soul, and Anselme's heart melted. They were sad and joyful at the same time: sad to abandon the initiator, joyful at what he had given them, and the new life that he had opened before them.

The road rose; the fourfold crossroads was in the distance, at the top of a high hill, and it was several hours after their departure when they arrived. A shelter stood in the very center of the plateau; they took refuge there. The philosopher laid Irène down gently on a bed of straw that was there. He remained leaning over her for a moment, protecting her slumber; then he straightened up and summoned the two young men.

They drew nearer to him and he asked them, in a low voice: "Don't you regret having met me?"

They tried to respond, but he stopped them. "There's still time," he said. "You can stop at the very entrance to the quarry. Look behind you; there's a good life in indifference and peace, untroubled by importunate sobs, devoid of chagrins and pains: an egotistical and tranquil life."

"Show us what there is ahead of us," Anselme interjected, "not what we're leaving behind."

"Is that what you want?"

"We want that," they both replied.

"So be it. Listen to me once more."

He stood up, and bent over Irène again. She was profoundly asleep. He came back to sit beside Claude and Anselme, and he spoke.

XXVIII

The Holocaust

ILARION was a sad adolescent. He lived in a miserable and remote quarter of a great city, where everyone knew him and liked him because he was handsome and melancholy. He was tall and slim, his face was a mat white with a slight yellow tint, like ivory that is beginning to age: the face of those whose hearts torment them. He had dark eyes, widely divided, the profundity of which was evident: eyes that looked inside his being. His brown hair, silky and curly, descended over his neck and shoulders, and his thin and nobly designed mouth seduced the women whom his eyes had not conquered. But Hilarion was insensible to the charm of women; he loved too much to desire, and could not limit his tenderness to a single individual.

He was unhealthily loving, to the point of excess, to the point of puerility—a puerility that sometimes impelled him to put as high a price on the suffering of an insect as that of his fellows. If he took pleasure in the joys of humans, he was delightfully stirred by their chagrins; at the spectacle of another's woe, warm waves of pity, affection and sympathy agitated his breast, and he experienced an infinite sweetness in shedding tears. As soon as he had wept, however, he sensed an anguish grip him, because he did not know how to calm those dolors.

As he grew older, the strange voluptuousness that invaded him when he saw someone suffering diminished and disappeared; he no longer understood the delight of tears; he knew their bitterness, and soon nothing resided within him but an immense universal love and a bitter sentiment of his impotence in the face of evil.

When he was twenty years old, he resolved to travel. One morning, he quit the house where he had been born and set forth. For years he traveled through hamlets and burgs, villages and cities. He was seen everywhere that human creatures were groaning: in the hovels where human wrecks run aground; in the mines where spines are curbed; in the factories where hair falls out, eyes are burned, teeth are pitted, bones soften, limbs are prey to paralysis and flesh the target of poisons; in the workshops where young women and young men are devoured by miasmas, corroded by the acridity of vapors, breasts hollowed out, lungs excavated, hearts become horny and the skin scaly; in the fields where laborers struggle against the miserly earth, whipped by the wind that carries harmful dust, torn by frosts, corroded by the sun, furrowed by the rain; in the shacks and the mansards where the humble, the ashamed and the desolate live. Everywhere, Hilarion took his sadness, his pity, his despair and his love.

One evening, after a day spent visiting subterranean grottoes where miners extracted salt painfully, the bitter crystals of which bit into their skin, Hilarion sat down on the edge of a ditch and wanted to die, because his arms were too weak to sustain all the miseries that he had already seen. He remained there for a few hours, prostrate and moaning.

A sound of footsteps on the road caused him to raise his head. The night was clear, and he saw a man who stopped in front of him, saluted him and said to him: "Where are you going, Hilarion?"

Hilarion replied that he did not know, and that question revived his cares; he began sobbing again. Then the passer-by pointed with his finger at an old manor that stood on a distant hill.

"Go up there," he ordered. "When you arrive at the manor, knock twice on the door. Old Cyrille, the guardian of the threshold, will ask you who you are. Reply: 'I've come from among those who are weeping.' He'll open the door for you, and you'll go into the dwelling of desires."

Having spoken, the stranger saluted him again and then went away without looking back. Hilarion got up, tightened his belt, picked up the staff that he had thrown down and headed toward the ancient manor. He thought that it was close by, but he did not reach the plateau at the top of the hill until the evening of the fourth day after that encounter, and the sun was disappearing behind the violet and orange silks of the western horizon when he knocked on the door.

The batten opened, an old man appeared, and, on seeing Hilarion, asked: "Who are you, you who are knocking?"

"I've come from among those who are weeping," replied Hilarion.

"Enter among those who want to die," replied the old man. "Follow me, Hilarion."

"I'll follow you, Cyrille."

"You've seen the annunciator?" asked Cyrille.

"I've seen him."

Cyrille smiled sadly, and he made a sign to the man he had just introduced to walk beside him. They both traversed cold porticoes and vast deserted courtyards; then, finally, they penetrated into the manor. It was an immense dwelling divided into small rooms linked by narrow vestibules. Each of the rooms was populated by a dolorous but smiling crowd, and Hilarion recognized on the faces of those who were accumulated there the same dolors painted on the faces of the wretches he had left behind, but they were peaceful and serene dolors. He divined that they had consented to them.

For two days they wandered through the manor, and when the second dusk fell, Cyrille showed Hilarion out through the door opposite the one by which he had entered. Hilarion thought that his guide was about to abandon him; he uttered a loud cry, retained him by the robe and said: "Don't leave me, Cyrille; my soul is full of chagrin and anguish. Why did the unknown passer-by send me to you, if I was only going to find suffering and anguish?"

"Think about it for a moment," replied the old man. "I told you that you were entering among those who are dying, those who are dying voluntarily. You've found suffering equal to that which you left behind, you say? Yes, but that suffering is accepted, sought, and those who are subject to it, as well as to inevitable death, accept it in order to lighten the burden of the plaintive people you left behind in the distant valley. They are the blissful holocaust: those who give in order to diminish Evil."

Cyrille fell silent. As Hilarion remained pensive, he withdrew soundlessly and closed the door. Abruptly, however, Hilarion knocked again loudly, and shouted: "Cyrille, receive me among those who want to die."

The door opened again. Hilarion went back into the manor, and beside Hilarion he saw the annunciator, who was smiling. A profound joy penetrated his being, his face lit up, and his delight was so great that he did not hear Cyrille say to his companion: "Will evil always triumph, then? Is it necessary for the noblest of men, always to agonize, in order to preserve the humble from atrocious claws, or merely to bandage their wounds?"

The annunciator did not reply, but, as he descended the hill, no longer seen by Hilarion, he wept.

XXIX

Dawn

THE PHILOSOPHER'S voice died away in a lament; he drew Claude and Anselme toward him and hugged them for a long time.

"Understand me," he said to them, "and when you think about Hilarion, remember that it is not the death that matters but the life. Don't sacrifice yourself for evil, nor to conserve an unjust benefit for others. Don't teach the poor to be the voluntary victims of the rich, don't glorify the lamb, the eternal host; retain the gleams of energy. Strike, for Justice."

"Did you not say," asked Anselme, "that the holocausts accepted suffering and inevitable death in order to lighten the burden of those who are weeping?"

"Understand me. It's not the acceptance of your agony that can diminish the evil, but the fashion in which you have lived. Don't hold your throat out to the knife, but don't recoil before the swords; be able to perish in order to lead others and yourselves to be good, and that your death will be the exaltation of your life. Prepare the hour when no one will any longer be constrained, in order to realize the good, to make the abominable sacrifice of himself.

Overturn the bloody altars on which human beings offer their first-born to the idols that they have erected."

A sound of footsteps resonated on the road.

"Here comes Juste," said Marcus, and went to meet him.

"I've kept you waiting," declared the vagabond, as he came into the shelter, "but I've brought the full knapsack. You forgot it in Claude's house; I thought it would be good to go and fetch it. I've pillaged the larder and it's heavily laden; my punishment will be to carry it."

"You want to come with me?" said the philosopher. "Wouldn't you prefer to remain in Geronta?"

"Old Master, it's necessary for me to go too. I might have compromised Corax. In any case, fried fish already seems less good to me, and I definitely can't abide the bitter wine. Shall I also confess that I like you, and wouldn't abandon your company even for that of the pilgrim students. You're the only man who can understand my folly and my wisdom; if I weren't myself, I'd like to be you. Let's leave together, and let me cheer up the journey for you."

"Come, then, friend; I'll also be glad to be buried by benevolent hands and when—soon, perhaps—you've closed my eyes, you can knock on Claude's door, and Claude will open his house to you."

"I don't like those morose ideas, Marcus, especially at a moment of departure; they darken the mood needlessly. The grave fault that I find in you is that of constantly mingling death into life, while I'd rather mingle life into death. But that's enough talk, and we have all the time in the world to resume the conversation. The sky is already paling, the dawn is precocious; let's salute our friends and pick up the staff."

Irène had woken up a moment before; she came to the old man and pressed herself against him.

"Adieu, my daughter," said the philosopher, "Adieu, dear heart that has opened to my voice. I confide her to you, Anselme. She's a frail plant over which it's necessary to watch. She'll know more doubt, sadness and despair; she'll be gripped by the fear of acting. Let your support never be lacking, and if she goes astray, show her the light that she has already seen shining."

He drew her to him tenderly, and slowly stroked her scattered hair.

"Adieu, Claude," he said. "Adieu, Anselme. Like the Solitary, return to the vineyard that it's necessary not to quit. Do your work in your own way; never let my memory be an obstacle to you; forget me rather than stop in your march. I love you, Claude, because you have given yourself to me, and I love you, Anselme, because I have conquered you. Go and conquer others. I have made the fire spring forth before you; don't let it go out. Be the torch-bearers, and transmit it, bright and burning, to those who will follow you, as those who preceded me handed on the torch to me. For you I could have commented further on my parables, made my myths and symbols more precise. I did not want to do that. I have a horror of dogmas and rules, and I would have been afraid of binding you in dangerous chains. I have removed the scales from your eyes, seek in the depths of your being now, and you will be able to find the truth there."

He fell silent, and his gaze seemed to be following an invisible cortege.

"I'm seeing again the morning of my life," he continued, "your young soul is entering into mine. How distant it is, and how close is the moment when my arm rose up against all oppression! What a breath of love and revolt filled my being, and what an immense hope penetrated me!

Now, in my decline, in spite of the inevitable temporary weaknesses, I have the same thoughts, the same hope, and the shadow into which I am entering is illuminated for me by daylight. Do as I have done; let your mature years know the joys of labor and let your old age be unaware of lassitude. If, when you are on the threshold of night, the work is not accomplished, maintain the young and vivacious hope regardless. The work will be done, and the hour will come when Justice will reign."

He embraced them all, and as Irène's eyes filled with tears, he begged her not to weep. "Let the day of my departure be a day of delight," he said. "When I came, you were plunged in darkness, I am going and the light is shining for you; let your heart be joyful; here comes the new dawn."

The sun rose.

From the hilltop, the silver ribbon of the river was visible, flowing majestically through the meadows. The yellow light of dawn gilded the proud hill in the distance, the flower-beds of which were shivering around the marble villas. The factory chimneys had extinguished their flames, and they were vomiting clouds of thick black smoke over the city of the poor. A dull rumble came from the city, from the docks that were awakening, the streets of the suburbs swarming at this hour with the matinal crowd going to work. On the horizon, the island could be distinguished, the giant arches of the bridges, the massive towers of the Palace, and the trees of the Garden of Speech.

With a broad gesture, the philosopher showed them Geronta. Once again he hugged his friends in his arms, and then he extracted himself from their grip.

Followed by Juste, he started walking westwards.

A PARTIAL LIST OF SNUGGLY BOOKS

LÉON BLOY *The Tarantulas' Parlor and Other Unkind Tales*

S. HENRY BERTHOUD *Misanthropic Tales*

FÉLICIEN CHAMPSAUR *The Latin Orgy*

FÉLICIEN CHAMPSAUR *The Emerald Princess and Other Decadent Fantasies*

BRENDAN CONNELL *Clark*

QUENTIN S. CRISP *Blue on Blue*

LADY DILKE *The Outcast Spirit and Other Stories*

BERIT ELLINGSEN *Vessel and Solsvart*

EDMOND AND JULES DE GONCOURT *Manette Salomon*

RHYS HUGHES *Cloud Farming in Wales*

J.-K. HUYSMANS *Knapsacks*

JUSTIN ISIS *Divorce Procedures for the Hairdressers of a Metallic and Inconstant Goddess*

VICTOR JOLY *The Unknown Collaborator and Other Legendary Tales*

BERNARD LAZARE *The Mirror of Legends*

JEAN LORRAIN *Masks in the Tapestry*

JEAN LORRAIN *Nightmares of an Ether-Drinker*

JEAN LORRAIN *The Soul-Drinker and Other Decadent Fantasies*

ARTHUR MACHEN *Ornaments in Jade*

CAMILLE MAUCLAIR *The Frail Soul and Other Stories*

CATULLE MENDÈS *Bluebirds*

LUIS DE MIRANDA *Who Killed the Poet?*

OCTAVE MIRBEAU *The Death of Balzac*

CHARLES MORICE *Babels, Balloons and Innocent Eyes*

DAMIAN MURPHY *Daughters of Apostasy*

KRISTINE ONG MUSLIM *Butterfly Dream*

YARROW PAISLEY *Mendicant City*

URSULA PFLUG *Down From*

JEAN RICHEPIN *The Bull-Man and the Grasshopper*

DAVID RIX *A Suite in Four Windows*

FREDERICK ROLFE *An Ossuary of the North Lagoon and Other Stories*

JASON ROLFE *An Archive of Human Nonsense*

BRIAN STABLEFORD *Spirits of the Vasty Deep*

BRIAN STABLEFORD (editor) *Decadence and Symbolism: A Showcase Anthology*

JANE DE LA VAUDÈRE *The Demi-Sexes and The Androgynes*

JANE DE LA VAUDÈRE *The Double Star and Other Occult Fantasies*

RENÉE VIVIEN *Lilith's Legacy*

KAREL VAN DE WOESTIJNE *The Dying Peasant*

THE TORCH-BEARERS

BERNARD LAZARE (1865–1903) was a French Jewish literary critic and journalist. Though mostly remembered today for his prominent role in the Dreyfus Affair and his book *Antisemitism: Its History and Causes*, he was also an important member of the Symbolist movement, and one of its purest and most extravagant exponents. He wrote drama and some poetry, but the core of his production consisted of an extensive sequence of short stories, or elaborated poems in prose, most of which he published in Symbolist periodicals between 1887 and 1893, and which he subsequently organized into three augmented collections. Although somewhat neglected today, for reasons that have nothing to do with their literary and philosophical merit, Lazare's short stories are key documents of the Symbolist movement, and a remarkable illustration of the methods and preoccupations of the writers whose activity constituted its heyday.

BRIAN STABLEFORD has been publishing fiction and non-fiction for fifty years. His fiction includes a series of "tales of the biotech revolution" and a series of metaphysical fantasies featuring Edgar Poe's Auguste Dupin. He is presently researching a history of French *roman scientifique* from 1700–1939 for Black Coat Press, translating much of the relevant material into English for the first time, and also translates material from the Decadent and Symbolist Movements. He has previously translated for Snuggly Books a number of titles, including *The Unknown Collaborator and Other Legendary Tales* by Victor Joly and *Bluebirds* by Catulle Mendès.